SOUTHERN BASTARDS

Volume 3

HOMECOMING

SOUTHERN BASTARDS, VOL 3: HOMECOMING. First printing. July 2016.

Published by Image Comics, Inc. Office of publication: 2001 Center Street, Sixth Floor, Berkeley, CA 94704. Originally published in single-magazine form as SOUTHERN BASTARDS #9-14.

Printed in the USA. For information regarding the CPSIA on this printed material call: 203-595-3636 and provide reference #RICH–558573. Representation: Law Offices of Harris M. Miller II, P.C. (rightsinquiries@gmail.com).
ISBN: 978-1-63215-610-5

SOUTHERN BASTARDS

"HOMECOMING"

created by
JASON AARON & JASON LATOUR

JASON AARON writer
(chapters 9-11, 13-14)

JASON LATOUR artist
(chapters 9-11, 13-14)

JASON LATOUR writer
(chapter 12)

CHRIS BRUNNER artist
(chapter 12)

JARED K. FLETCHER letters & design

SEBASTIAN GIRNER editor

Chapter 9

The One Who Never Got Away

THE CLOSER I GET TO 40, THE MORE CONVINCED I AM THAT THE BULK OF A MAN'S LIFE IS NOTHIN' BUT A SERIES OF ***UNIMPORTANT*** MOMENTS.

WE EAT, WE SLEEP, WE FUCK, WE WORK. WE WATCH TV. WE TALK AND TALK AND TALK.

SOME OF THOSE MOMENTS MIGHT SEEM IMPORTANT AT THE TIME, BUT IN THE END, THEY'RE MORE ***GRISTLE*** THAN MEAT.

JUST SHIT WE DO 'CAUSE WE'RE ALIVE AND WE GOTTA DO SOMETHIN' TO PASS THE TIME.

THE REALLY ***IMPORTANT*** MOMENTS COME ALONG ONCE IN A BLUE FUCKIN' MOON.

SOMETIMES YOU KNOW 'EM WHEN YOU'RE LIVIN' 'EM. SOMETIMES YOU DON'T SEE 'EM FOR WHAT THEY WAS UNTIL THEY'RE GONE.

THOSE BRIEF LITTLE MOMENTS OF RECKONING MAY SEEM ***SMALL*** WHEN YOU LOOK BACK OVER ALL YOUR DAYS.

BUT THOSE ARE THE MOMENTS THAT DECIDE WHAT KIND OF ***MAN*** YOU WAS WHEN YOU WALKED THIS EARTH.

THEY'RE THE MOMENTS YOU DON'T WANNA FUCK UP.

I'VE FUCKED UP EVERY ***LAST*** DAMN ONE OF MINE.

WHAT THE HELL KINDA MAN DOES THAT MAKE ***ME?***

SOUTHERN BASTARDS

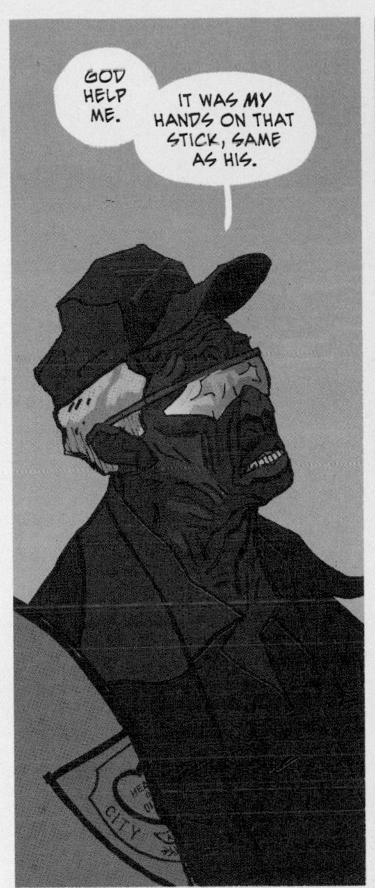
GOD HELP ME.
IT WAS MY HANDS ON THAT STICK, SAME AS HIS.

THAT AIN'T TRUE, COACH. THIS AIN'T YOUR FAULT.
AIN'T IT?
EULESS WOULD STILL BE LIVIN' IN A TRAILER IN THE WOODS IF IT WASN'T FOR MY STUPID ASS.
OR BURIED IN 'EM LIKE HIS DADDY.
I TOLD MYSELF ALL THESE YEARS I WAS KEEPIN' HIM IN CHECK. BUT THAT WAS JUST A LIE TO HELP ME SLEEP NIGHTS, WASN'T IT?
I'M TIRED A' LYIN.' SICK AND DAMN TIRED OF IT.

AIN'T YOU?
YOU WAS MEANT FOR BETTER THINGS THAN THIS, SON.
I'M SORRY I COULDN'T NEVER HELP YOU GET THERE.

BUT THE GOOD LORD ALWAYS GIVES US ANOTHER CHANCE, DON'T HE? I BELIEVE THAT WITH ALL MY HEART.
ANOTHER CHANCE TO MAKE THINGS RIGHT.
WE JUST GOTTA BE MAN ENOUGH TO TAKE IT.
YES, SIR. YES, WE DO.

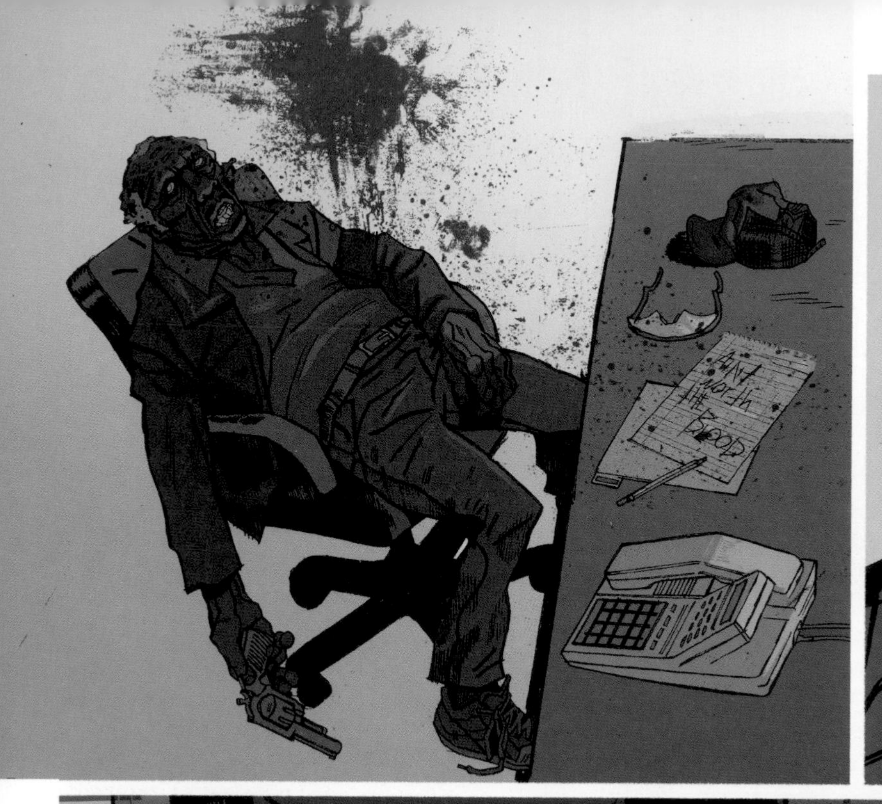

JESUS CHRIST.

YOU SEE WHAT THIS IS, DON'T YA?
I THINK... THAT'S PRETTY OBVIOUS.
DAMN RIGHT IT IS.

BIG WAS MURDERED.

MURDERED?

I DON'T SEE YOU AT THE GAMES MUCH NO MORE, SHERIFF, SO MAYBE YOU DON'T KNOW WHAT WEEK THIS IS.
IT'S HOMECOMING. AND YOU KNOW WHO WE PLAY FOR HOMECOMING THIS YEAR?
WETUMPKA COUNTY.

WHEN I FIRST GOT THIS JOB, EVERYBODY I'D SEE IN THE GROCERY STORE OR AT CHURCH ON SUNDAYS, EVEN THE LITTLE OLD BLUE-HAIRED LADIES, WOULD STOP AND TELL ME...
IT DIDN'T MATTER IF I WON EVERY OTHER GAME BY A HUNDRED POINTS, IF I COULDN'T BEAT WETUMPKA, I WOULDN'T HAVE MY JOB FOR LONG.

I HAVE BEATEN 'EM. NINETEEN STRAIGHT AT THIS POINT. 32 OUTTA' 39 TIMES, INCLUDIN' THE PLAYOFFS.
BIG WAS WITH ME FOR EVERY DAMN ONE A' THEM GAMES.

I DON'T CARE WHAT IT LOOKS LIKE, SHERIFF. HE WAS MURDERED.
AND MY GUT TELLS ME HIS KILLER COME FROM WETUMPKA.
BIG NEVER WOULDA DONE THIS TO HISSELF. ESPECIALLY NOT THIS WEEK. HE'D NEVER OF...

JUST FIND WHOEVER THE HELL DID THIS.

EVER THINK BACK TO SEX YOU HAD IN HIGH SCHOOL?
COUNTY 75th HOMECOMING
COMPSON BANK
RUN 'EM
REBS

HEY, THERE, SHERIFF. GONNA BE A CRAZY WEEK, AIN'T IT? YOU READY FOR THE BIG GAME?
YEAH. I RECKON SO.
EVER LOSE YOURSELF IN THAT MEMORY? RELIVE IT A BIT?
THEN STOP AND REALIZE YOU'RE A GROWN ASS MAN FANTASIZIN' 'BOUT A 17-YEAR-OLD GIRL?
I DO THAT EVERY DAMN DAY.

SURE WISH WE STILL HAD YOU OUT THERE RUNNIN' FOR THE REBS. WETUMPKA WOULDN'T STAND A CHANCE, WOULD THEY? YOU WAS THE BEST DANG BACK I EVER SEEN.
IT'S A SHAME WHAT HAPPENED TO YOUR LEG, IT SURELY IS. I SURE DO WISH YOU COULD'VE--
EXCUSE ME.

IT AIN'T THAT I'M SOME PERVERT LIKES LUSTIN' AFTER TEENAGE GIRLS.
IT'S JUST I'M A GUY WHO PEAKED TOO DAMN EARLY IS ALL.
A MAN WHO LIVES IN THE SHADOW OF THE BOY HE WAS.
TING

COMPSON BANK

AND THE GIRL WHO LOVED HIM.
MORNIN', MS. COMPSON.

GOOD MORNING, SHERIFF.
I NEED TO SEE MY SAFE DEPOSIT BOX, IF YOU PLEASE.
OF COURSE. RIGHT THIS WAY.

HOW YOU BEEN?

HOW'S YOUR SISTER THESE DAYS?
I DON'T SEE Y'ALL AT CHURCH MUCH ANYMORE.
LISTEN... YOU THINK MAYBE WE COULD--
CLUNG

EVERYTHING THERE?
LOOKS LIKE.
GOOD. NOW TAKE IT AND FIND SOME OTHER BANK TO KEEP IT IN.

GOODBYE, SHERIFF.

HARDY...
DON'T STOP. DON'T EVER--

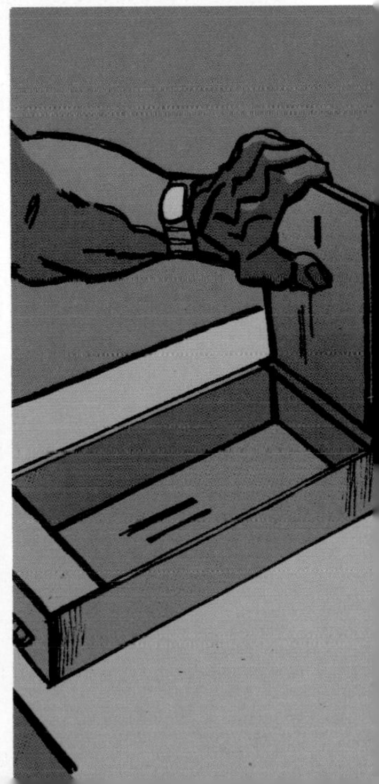

ON THE FIELD, I WAS A MAN AMONG BOYS.
SHIT
I STIFF-ARMED LINEBACKERS. PUNISHED SAFETIES. OUTRAN CORNERS.
EVEN WHEN EVERYBODY IN THE STADIUM KNEW I WAS GETTIN' THE BALL, THE OTHER TEAM STILL COULDN'T STOP IT.
EVERYBODY SAID I HAD SOMETHIN' YOU COULDN'T TEACH. SOMETHIN' YOU HAD TO BE BORN WITH.
A GIFT.
ONE THAT WAS GONNA TAKE ME FAR.
AS FAR AS I WANTED TO GO.

WHICH WAS ALL THE DAMN WAY.
COACH?
YOU WANTED TO SEE ME?

HEARD YOU GOT ANOTHER SCHOLARSHIP OFFER.
YES, SIR. OLE MISS THIS TIME.
HOW MANY'S THAT NOW?
I CAN'T RIGHTLY SAY, COACH. ELEVEN OR TWELVE, I RECKON.

I WAS GONNA...ASK YOU FOR HELP IN PICKIN' ONE.
OH, I'D BE HAPPY TO HELP, HARDY. ALWAYS HAVE BEEN, HAVEN'T I?
YES, SIR.
HOW IS YOUNG MS. COMPSON THESE DAYS?

SHE'S... FINE, SIR. HER AND HER SISTER BOTH.
THAT'S GOOD. IT'S GOOD THEY DIDN'T LET ALL THAT UNPLEASANTNESS GET TO 'EM.
AND IT WAS UNPLEASANT, WASN'T IT?

A DEATH IN THE FAMILY ALWAYS IS.

COACH... I AIN'T NEVER SAID A WORD TO **NOBODY** ABOUT THAT NIGHT. NOT EVEN MY MOMMA.
AND I NEVER WILL.
JUST LIKE I PROMISED YA.

I BELIEVE YOU, HARDY. I TRUST YOU. ALWAYS DID. WOULDN'T HAVE HELPED YOU IF I DIDN'T.
THANK YOU, SIR.
YOU'RE ONE OF THE BEST PLAYERS EVER COME THROUGH HERE. BETTER THAN **ME** EVEN, AND I DON'T SAY THAT OFTEN.
IT'S JUST A **SHAME** WHAT HAPPENED TO YOUR LEG.

MY LEG?
COACH, AIN'T **NOTHIN'** WRONG WITH MY LEG.

YOU **SURE** 'BOUT THAT?

ESAW? MATERHEAD? WHAT IS THIS?
HEY, HARDY. I'M REAL SORRY TO HEAR ABOUT YOUR LEG.

COACH, I DON'T UNDERSTAND. DID I DO SOMETHING WRONG?
I DID YOU A FAVOR, SON. I HELPED YOU WHEN YOU NEEDED IT MOST. HELPED YOU WHEN NOBODY ELSE IN THIS COUNTY WOULD'VE DARED.
YOU DON'T RETURN THAT FAVOR BY RUNNIN' OFF TO COLLEGE AND NEVER COMIN' BACK.

WHAT... WHAT ARE YOU SAYIN'?
I NEVER PLAYED COLLEGE BALL NEITHER. AND I WAS STRONGER FOR IT.

YOU WILL BE TOO.

THE MOST IMPORTANT RUN OF MY LIFE...
AND I DIDN'T EVEN MAKE IT FIVE YARDS.
KRAK
HRRGH
I GOT BIG PLANS FOR YOU, HARDY. TELL ME, SON...
GAAARGH! FUCK! STOP!
THUNT
THUNT
HOW DOES "SHERIFF" SOUND?
AARRGH!
THUNT

WARRIOR
COUNTRY
WELCOME TO
WETUMPKA
COUNTY, ALABAMA
IT'S A SCHOOL NIGHT, BOYS. SHOULDN'T Y'ALL BE HOME STUDYIN' YOUR PLAYBOOK?
GET OUT THE GODDAMN WAY, SHERIFF! WE AIN'T GONE LET THEM FUCKERS GET AWAY WITH IT!
THEM SONS A BITCHES FROM WETUMPKA KILLED COACH BIG!
WE GONE BURN THEIR GODDAMN SCHOOL DOWN!

I SEE LINEBACKERS, SAFETIES, LINEMEN. SOME CAPTAINS EVEN. Y'ALL REALLY THINK BIG WOULD WANT HIS DEFENSE DOIN' SHIT LIKE THIS THE WEEK OF A GAME?
IF Y'ALL WANNA HONOR YOUR COACH, YOU'LL GO HOME, GET SOME SLEEP AND PLAY YOUR ASS OFF COME FRIDAY.

IS THAT WHAT YOU'RE DOIN' OUT HERE, SHERIFF? HONORIN' BIG? OR HIDIN' IN THE FUCKIN' DARK?
WHERE'S HIS FUCKIN' KILLER, SHERIFF?

NOT IN WETUMPKA, THAT'S FOR DAMN SURE.
YOU BOYS ARE RILED UP AND HALF LIT. AND I AIN'T IN THE MOOD FOR THIS SHIT TONIGHT.
IT'S HOMECOMIN' WEEK. SO GO THE FUCK HOME, REBS.
THAT AIN'T GONNA HAPPEN, IS IT?
WHAT THE FUCK YOU THINK, SHERIFF?

I THINK IT'S BEEN TOO DAMN LONG SINCE I WHOOPED A LINEBACKER'S ASS.

BOSS BBQ
HAVE YOU LOST YOUR FUCKING MIND?

RIGHT NOW, I'M DRUNK ENOUGH THAT I AIN'T FOR SURE.

WHY DID I JUST GET A CALL THAT YOU ARRESTED HALF MY STARTIN' DEFENSE?
'CAUSE I DID.
DON'T WORRY, THEY'RE FINE. A BIT BUMPED AND BRUISED AND HUMBLED, MAYBE. YOU CAN BAIL 'EM OUT IN ABOUT AN HOUR.

YOU ARE GONNA TURN RIGHT THE FUCK AROUND AND GO GET THEM--
I AIN'T DOIN' NO SUCH THING.

IT WAS SUICIDE.

ANY GODDAMN FOOL COULD SEE THAT.
BIG BLEW HIS OWN BRAINS OUT.
SHUT YOUR FUCKIN' MOUTH. BIG WOULD NEVER--
AND HE DID IT BECAUSE A' YOU.

BECAUSE OF WHAT YOU MADE THAT POOR MAN INTO. THE SHIT YOU MADE HIM A PARTY TO.
HE WAS ASHAMED AND DISGUSTED BY IT. BY YOU AND **EVERYTHING** YOU EVER--

DON'T WORRY, BOSS. I KNOW MY **JOB.**
I GET PAID TO LOOK THE OTHER WAY. I'M GOOD AS HELL AT DOIN' THAT.
AND I'LL **KEEP ON** DOIN' IT. WHAT THE FUCK ELSE AM I GONNA DO AROUND HERE?

YOU WANNA KILL ME OR SOMETHIN', HELL, I'LL BE EASY ENOUGH TO FIND.
I'LL BE THERE **FRIDAY NIGHT** JUST LIKE EVERY-BODY ELSE.

GOOD LUCK AGAINST WETUMPKA, COACH.
WITHOUT BIG... YOU'RE SURE AS HELL GONNA **NEED** IT.

FOR A SECOND THERE I THOUGHT... MAYBE THIS WAS GONNA BE ANOTHER ONE A' THEM MOMENTS LIKE I WAS TALKIN' ABOUT.
THE IMPORTANT KIND.

CROOKED COP FINALLY STANDS UP AND DOES THE RIGHT THING. I LOVE THOSE MOVIES.
BUT THAT AIN'T WHAT JUST HAPPENED, IS IT?
ONLY PEOPLE I ARRESTED TONIGHT WERE SOME DRUNK KIDS. AND NOW I'M DRUNKER THAN THEY WAS.
CITY
POLICE

WHAT YOU'RE LOOKIN' AT RIGHT NOW IS A MAN WHO'S FINALLY GIVEN THE FUCK UP ON EVERYTHIN'. EVEN LIFE.
A MAN MADE OF NOTHIN' BUT SOME FADED OLD MEMORIES. MEMORIES NOBODY BUT HIM EVEN WANTS TO REMEMBER.

A MAN WITH NOTHIN' LEFT TO HIS NAME THAT HE GIVES TWO SHITS ABOUT.

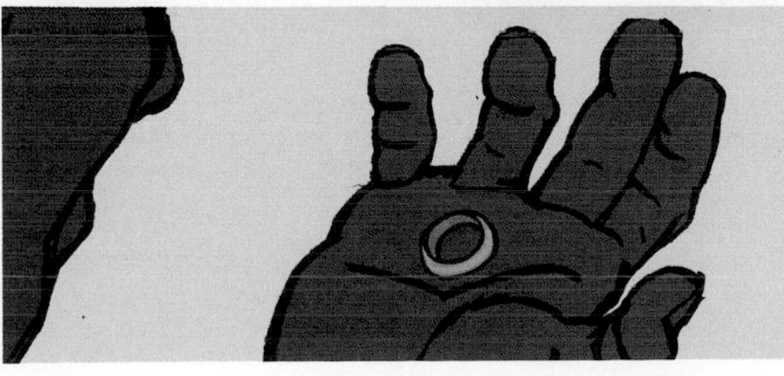

NOTHIN' AT ALL.
DADDY!

Chapter 10

The Gospel According to Esaw Goings

HOT GARBAGE. DIRTY FUCKIN' BABY DIAPERS. DEAD ROTTEN DOG ON THE SIDE OF 78.
SOCCER.
DON'T CUM YET. DON'T CUM YET. DON'T...
HNF
ESAW! THERE'S SOMEBODY HERE WHO WANTS TO SAVE YOUR SOUL!
DO FUCKIN' WHAT NOW?!

THE NIGHT BEFORE.
"WHEN YOU SAW ONLY ONE SET OF FOOTPRINTS...
IT WAS THEN THAT I CARRIED YOU."
SHELBY ANNE. THE LORD'S DONE LAID A **BURDEN** ON MY HEART.

I AIN'T DOIN' ENOUGH TO SPREAD HIS WORD.
DONNY RAY, BABY, THAT JUST AIN'T TRUE. NOBODY AT NEW HOPE GOES WITNESSIN' MORE THAN YOU.
I TALK TO FOLKS WHO COME TO CHURCH ON SUNDAY MORNINGS ABOUT COMING BACK ON WEDNESDAYS. OR TALK TO KIDS ABOUT NOT TEXTIN' NAKED PICTURES OF THEIRSELVES.
JESUS MINISTERED TO LEPERS AND WHORES.

I DON'T BELIEVE WE GOT NO WHORES IN CRAW COUNTY. UNLESS YOU MEAN THAT RAGLAND GIRL THAT ALWAYS WEARS SHORTS TO FELLOWSHIP.
I NEED TO SHARE THE LORD'S GOSPEL WITH THEM WHAT NEEDS IT THE MOST.
BUT...*WHO*, BABY? WHO YOU TALKING ABOUT?
WELL... *ONE NAME* DOES COME TO MIND.

ESAW! YOU COMIN'?!

ALMOST!
UGGGH! FUUUUCK! AAAAHHH, FUCK YEAH!

UGGHH! UGGGGGH!
HE'LL BE OUT IN A MINUTE.
FUCK YEAH! FUCK THAT--!
SHIT! AAHHH! AHHH!
HUUGGGHH!

WOULD YOU MIND IF I READ TO YOU FROM THE BOOK OF THE LORD?
OH, THAT'S OKAY. I GO TO SUNDAY SCHOOL AT FIRST BAPTIST.

REBEL
WHO THE FUCK IS THIS?

I'M...
HE'S FROM CHURCH.
CHURCH?

MY DADDY SENT YA, HUH. WELL YOU CAN TELL HIM TO FUCK THE HELL OFF.
YOU A FED OR SOMETHIN'? STATE POLICE?
I DON'T GO TO YOUR DADDY'S CHURCH. I GO TO--
NO. I'M JUST HERE TO TALK ABOUT...ABOUT GOD'S PLAN FOR YOU, ESAW.
DOP

HEH. YOU SERIOUS?
HEH HEH HEH.
WELL SHIT. COME ON THEN, BITCH.
LET'S HEAR WHAT THE MOTHERFUCKER'S GOT IN MIND.

SOUTHERN BASTARDS

THE BIBLE SAYS...THERE'S ALWAYS TIME TO GET RIGHT WITH THE LORD. NO MATTER HOW WE'VE SINNED, HE'S ALWAYS--
HOLD THAT THOUGHT. GOTTA MAKE A QUICK STOP.
COMPSON BAN
NEED TO MAKE A WITHDRAWAL. FROM THE FOOTBALL FUND.
TITTIES.

BOYS NEED NEW PADS.
TITTIES.
HOW MUCH?
$300,000 OUGHTTA DO IT. PADS IS SURE EXPENSIVE THESE DAYS.
TITTIES. TITTIES. TITTIES.

WHO'S HE?
HE'S WITH ME.
WHY IS HE SWEATING LIKE HE'S ABOUT TO ROB THE PLACE?
HE'S NEW.

"NEW" MAKES ME NERVOUS. LIKE I'VE TOLD COACH BOSS--
HOW 'BOUT YOU JUST GET THE MONEY, MS. COMPSON? OKAY?
BITCH. UPPITY FUCKING BITCH.
TITTIES.

ASS. ASS. FUCK THAT ASS. FUCK THAT--
YOU WANT ME TO COME WITH YA?
NO. WAIT HERE.

SOMEDAY.
YOU GOT ANY BITCHES AT HOME, BIBLE BOY?
I...I HAVE A WIFE. AND MY NAME IS--
BET SHE AIN'T GOT NO ASS LIKE THAT.
TELL THE TRUTH... YOU'D TRADE ALL THE BULLSHIT IN THAT LITTLE BOOK OF YOURS TO CLIMB UP INSIDE THAT PUSSY JUST ONE TIME, WOULDN'T YA?
REBEL
SHIT

SHIT, I'D TRADE MY MOMMA'S EYEBALLS FOR SOME OF THAT ASS.
OR BETTER YET, HER TWIN SISTER'S ASS. HELL, THE SISTER'S PRACTICALLY A DAMN VIRGIN, AIN'T SHE? 'LESS THEIR DADDY COUNTS. HEH.
ESAW...
REBEL
SHIT HAPPENS

AFTER THIS, DO YOU THINK MAYBE WE COULD...TAKE A MOMENT TO TALK IN PRIVATE...ABOUT THE PLAN GOD HAS FOR EACH OF US. AND ABOUT HOW CAN WE CAN SEE HIM IN--
YOU WANNA SEE GOD?
WWJD

SHIT, WHY DIDN'T YA SAY SO?
LET'S GO SEE GOD.
REBEL

COACH?
I WENT BY THE BANK AND GOT THE MONEY FOR TONIGHT. I'M GONNA MEET THEM MOBILE BOYS OUT AT--
WHO THE HELL IS THAT?
AH, HE AIN'T NOBODY.
THEN WHY THE FUCK IS HE HERE?
LIKE I SAID, I'M GONE MEET THEM MOBILE BOYS TONIGHT AND I JUST FIGURED I MIGHT NEED ME SOME--
STOP TALKING.

I DON'T KNOW WHAT THE FUCK YOU'RE GOIN' ON ABOUT. I JUST KNOW IT AIN'T FOOTBALL.
I'M TALKIN' ABOUT MOBILE, COACH, YOU KNOW, AND THEM FELLAS WITH THE--
GODDAMNIT, ESAW. HOW FUCKIN' RETARDED ARE YOU?
IT'S THE WEEK OF THE BIGGEST DAMN GAME OF THE YEAR. AND MY DEFENSIVE COORDINATOR JUST UP AND FUCKIN' DIED. DO YOU REALLY THINK I GIVE TWO SHITS ABOUT ANYTHING ELSE RIGHT NOW?
NO, SIR.
YOU WANNA BE OF SOME FUCKIN' USE, GO DRAW ME UP A NEW GODDAMN DEFENSIVE GAMEPLAN.
YOU... YOU SERIOUS, COACH? 'CAUSE I CAN DO THAT. I BEEN TELLIN' YOU FOR YEARS THAT I CAN...
HOLY SHIT.
AT FUCKIN' LAST.
IT'S TIME. TIME TO UNLEASH HELL.

MATERHEAD! WHERE THE FUCK ARE YOU?
BOSS BBQ
YOU GOTTA HELP ME UNLEASH HELL. I MEAN...
JUST CALL ME BACK, DAMN IT.
REBEL
SHIT

JESUS. SINCE WHEN DO YOU NEED SO MANY FUCKIN' BOOKS TO PLAY FOOT-BALL?
WAP
WAP
WAP
WE'LL JUST... WE'LL BLITZ 'EM. WE'LL BLITZ THE SHIT OUT OF 'EM THE WHOLE FUCKIN' GAME.
RIGHT UP THE DAMN MIDDLE WITH THE LINEBACKERS. GET RIGHT IN THE QUARTERBACK'S FACE. HE WON'T HAVE TIME TO...

IF YOU'RE GONNA RUSH BOTH INSIDE LINEBACKERS, YOU BETTER BRING DOWN A SAFETY TO COVER THE CROSSING ROUTE.
HOLY BIBLE

WHAT?
FUCK YOU. GO BACK TO READING YOUR...
HE'S RIGHT.

YOU GONE HAVE TO MIX IT UP OR THEY'LL HIT A BIG ONE RIGHT OVER THE TOP OF YA.
MAYBE RUN SOME ZONE BLITZ, IF YOU FIGURE YOUR LINEMEN CAN DROP INTO--

GODDAMNIT! FOOTBALL AIN'T ABOUT X'S AND FUCKIN' O'S AND SHIT!
IT'S ABOUT WHO FUCKIN' WANTS IT THE MOST!
IT'S ABOUT LININ' UP ACROSS FROM YOUR MAN AND BEATIN' HIS FUCKIN' ASS INTO THE TURF, NO MATTER WHAT GODDAMN PLAY IS CALLED!

WE'RE CRAW FUCKIN' COUNTY. AND THEY AIN'T.
THAT'S MY MOTHERFUCKIN' GAMEPLAN.

C'MON, BIBLE BITCH, WE GOT SOMEWHERE TO BE.
IT'S GETTIN' ROUND ABOUT SUPPER TIME NOW, ESAW, AND WELL, WE STILL AIN'T HAD MUCH TIME TO TALK ABOUT THE LORD.
MAYBE WE OUGHTTA TRY AGAIN TOMORROW.

THERE'S ONLY ONE REASON I BROUGHT YOUR ASS WITH ME TODAY, ASSHOLE. AND THIS IS IT.
GET IN THE FUCKIN' CAR.

DON'T SAY SHIT, YOU HEAR ME?

AND DON'T FUCKIN' MOVE FROM THAT SPOT.
NO MATTER WHAT HAPPENS.
WHAT... WHAT IS HAPPENING? I DON'T...
SHIT HAPPE
Rele

I SAID SHUT THE FUCK UP. I'LL DO THE TALKIN'.

EVENIN', BOYS. HOW WAS THE DRIVE?
REBEL

Y'ALL HAVE ANY PROBLEMS ALONG THE WAY?
GOT YOUR MONEY RIGHT HERE. WHAT Y'ALL GOT FOR ME THIS WEEK?

A WARNING.

DON'T EVER DO THIS SHIT AGAIN.
DO WHAT? I'M JUST TRYIN' TO CONDUCT BUSINESS, SAME AS--

DON'T BRING SOME SCARED LITTLE CIVILIAN OUT HERE WITH YA, JUST TO TRY AND CONVINCE US YOU'RE SO FUCKING HARD, SO GODDAMN CRAZY...
YOU CAN BRING ANY DAMN BITCH IN THE WORLD WITH YOU AS BACK-UP.

OR AM I READING IT WRONG? AND *YOU'RE* THE BITCH. AND HE'S THE CRAZY ONE.
...
WHERE'S THE FUCKIN' GUNS?

THIS SHIT AIN'T PROFESSIONAL, ESAW. BEST GET IT TOGETHER, BOY.

OR WE GONE HAVE TO HAVE A WORD WITH THE COACH.

SPEED
KEEP
Alabam
Beautiful
NO DUMPING

TAT AT TAT
TAT AT TAT
TAT AT TAT
TAT AT TAT
SHIT HAPPENS

TAT AT TAT
SHIT HAPPENS

AT AT TAT

I SHOULD REALLY BE--
PICK UP ONE A' THEM GUNS.

I CAN'T...
PICK IT UP AND SHOOT THAT SIGN OVER THERE.
I...I'VE NEVER...

PICK IT THE FUCK UP.

NO.

I BET YOU WANNA PICK THAT SHIT UP NOW, DON'T YA?
NO. PLEASE, I...I...
HOW 'BOUT NOW?

OR NOW?
OR MAYBE NOW?
HOW MANY OTHER CHEEKS YOU GOT LEFT TO TURN, HUH? C'MON, BITCH!
AH YEAH, **THERE** YOU GO. **NOW** YOU WANT THAT SHIT, DON'T YOU?
THAT'S RIGHT, PICK IT UP! SHOW ME HOW FULL A' SHIT YOU ARE! HOW YOU'RE JUST THE SAME AS...
THE LORD IS...IS MY SHEPHERD...
WHAT YOU GONNA DO? YOU GONNA WAVE YOUR FUCKIN' GOOD BOOK AT ME? HUH? JUST LIKE MY DADDY?
YOU THINK YOU GONE MAKE ME CRY AGAIN, PREACHIN' ABOUT HELL AND DEMONS AND SHIT?
I AIN'T SCARED NO MORE, DADDY.
I'M THE FUCKIN' DEMON NOW.
AIN'T I? FUCKIN' SAY IT.
SAY I'M A DEMON. SAY IT.
YOU CAME TO SAVE MY FUCKIN' SOUL.
WELL HERE'S YOUR BIG GODDAMN CHANCE.
HOLD THAT BIBLE OVER YOUR FACE.
PLEASE... ESAW...I JUST... I JUST CAME TO...
WHAT...?

PUT IT OVER YOUR FUCKIN' FACE!

JESUS. OH, JESUS.
YOU THINK THAT BOOK HAS TO POWER TO SAVE, HUH?

LET'S SEE IF YOU'RE RIGHT.

THAK THAK
THAK
THAK
THAK

HEY, 'SAW. IT'S MATER.
I THOUGHT WE WAS GONE WORK ON THIS DEFENSIVE GAMEPLAN?
I GOT SOME... QUESTIONS ABOUT SOME OF THESE BLITZES YOU DREW UP. CALL ME BACK, ALL RIGHT?
AT TAT
TAT AT TA
SHELBY ANNE?
DONNY RAY? OH THANK GOD. WHAT TIME IS IT, BABY? WHERE HAVE YOU...

TAT AT TAT
TAT AT

DONNY RAY... OH MY GOD...
THE LORD'S... DONE LAID ANOTHER BURDEN... ON MY HEART...

AT TAT
TAT AT

THE LORD WANTS US TO MOVE.
FUCK YOU.
FUCK YOU.
FUCK YOU.
FUCK YOU.
FUCK YOU.
FUCK YOU TOO.

Chapter 11

You're Lookin' at Country

I'VE LIVED ALL MY LIFE IN CRAW COUNTY, ALABAMA, AND BELIEVE IT OR NOT...
I DON'T GIVE A DAMN ABOUT FOOTBALL.
HEAVENLY FATHER, THANK YOU FOR THIS BLESSING.

AIN'T BEEN TO A GAME SINCE I WAS A KID.
DON'T GO INTO TOWN AT ALL UNLESS I GOT TO. DON'T LIKE TO LEAVE THE WOODS.
DON'T NEED TO. A MAN'S GOT ALL HE NEEDS RIGHT HERE. IF HE'S ANY SORTA MAN AT ALL.
MY DADDY TAUGHT ME HOW TO HUNT THESE WOODS. WITH A BOW AND NOTHING ELSE. WE **BOONES** HAVE ALWAYS BEEN BOWHUNTERS.
SITTING IN A HEATED DEER BLIND, WAITING FOR A BUCK TO WANDER UP AND EAT THE CLOVER YOU PLANTED SO YOU CAN BLAST IT WITH A SHOTGUN...THAT AIN'T HUNTIN'.
MIGHT AS WELL GO TO THE PIGGLY WIGGLY.
AIN'T NO PIGGLY WIGGLY OUT HERE.

YOU'LL FIND PLENTY A' FOLKS IN TOWN WHO HUNT WITH LASER SCOPES AND STORE-BOUGHT DEER SCENTS AND LIVE IN BIG NEW HOUSES DOWN THE STREET FROM THE WAL-MART...
BUT STILL WANNA TALK ABOUT HOW BACKWOODS AND *COUNTRY* THEY ARE.

MY GRANNY'S 85 YEARS OLD AND STILL HOES HER OWN GARDEN. STILL QUILTS AND CANS EVEN THOUGH HER HANDS ARE ALL GNARLED FROM ARTHRITIS.
SHE AIN'T NEVER LIVED ON NO PAVED ROAD. AIN'T NEVER OWNED NO AIR CONDITIONER.
THAT THERE'S COUNTRY.

MY GRANDDADDY BUILT THIS CABIN WITH HIS OWN HANDS. CHOPPED EVERY LOG. HAMMERED EVERY NAIL.
HE WAS A COAL MINER. DIED OF THE BLACK LUNG.
MY DADDY DIED BUILDING THE DOOLEY DAM. HE'S BURIED SOMEWHERE AT THE BOTTOM OF THAT LAKE, DOWN WHERE THERE'S CATFISH THE SIZE OF CARS.

MY MOMMA PICKED COTTON AND CHURNED HER OWN BUTTER AND DIED THE DAY I WAS BORN.
I DON'T KNOW THE FIRST DAMN THING ABOUT FOOTBALL AND DON'T RIGHTLY CARE, BUT I KNOW COUNTRY.
COUNTRY'S ALL I'VE EVER KNOWN.

SHLUNK
THERE WERE BOONES WHO DIED AT SHILOH AND VICKSBURG. THEY WERE ALL TOO POOR TO OWN SLAVES. THEY JUST HATED YANKEES.

SSSSSSSH
AND LOVED THE WOODS WHERE THEY WAS BORN. LOVED 'EM ENOUGH TO KILL FOR 'EM.

SPULCH
IMAGINE THAT.

AIN'T NO RED LIGHTS IN PINEY WOODS.
THERE'S JUST A BAIT SHOP AND A TIN-ROOF BBQ SHACK AND A BUNCH A' OLD LOGGIN' ROADS.
WHICH IS JUST THE WAY WE LIKE IT.
PINEY WOOD HOLINESS CHURCH OF GOD.
JESUS IS COMING SOON WE DONT KNOW THE DAY OR THE H UR
"AND WHEN THE DAY OF PENTECOST WAS FULLY COME, THEY WERE ALL WITH ONE ACCORD IN ONE PLACE."
"AND SUDDENLY THERE CAME A SOUND FROM HEAVEN AS OF A RUSHING MIGHTY WIND, AND IT FILLED ALL THE HOUSE WHERE THEY WERE SITTING.
"AND THERE APPEARED UPON THEM CLOVEN TONGUES AS OF FIRE, AND IT SAT UPON EACH OF THEM."
PRAISE THE LORD! YES, SIR!
they shall cast out devils;
hall speak with new tongues;
shall take up serpents;
deadly thing, shall
not hurt them;

"AND THEY WERE ALL FILLED WITH THE HOLY GHOST AND BEGAN TO SPEAK WITH OTHER TONGUES, AS THE SPIRIT GAVE THEM UTTERANCE."
SHANNA SHANDALAH LO MAKKA MADALAH ANNA!
YES, LORD!
PRAISE JESUS! PRAISE HIS NAME!
HALLA MADALALLAH!

"AND THESE SIGNS SHALL FOLLOW THEM THAT BELIEVE," SAID THE RISEN LORD.
AMEN?
"IN MY NAME SHALL THEY CAST OUT DEVILS. THEY SHALL SPEAK WITH NEW TONGUES."
AMEN!
"THEY SHALL TAKE UP SERPENTS!"
HALLELUJAH!

AIN'T NO GIANT MEGA-CHURCHES IN PINEY WOODS NEITHER.
OUT HERE WE'RE ALL HOLY GHOSTERS AND HOLY ROLLERS.
OUT HERE WE KNOW WHAT IT REALLY TAKES TO GET RIGHT WITH THE LORD.
I FEEL IT! I'M FILLED WITH THE SPIRIT! I'M READY TO...

GAAARGGHH!

TOMMY!
TOMMY GOT BIT!
NO.
OH, LORD JESUS, GET HIM UP AND--

HE'S IN THE LORD'S HANDS NOW.

NNGGGHH. JESUS. IT BURNS. IT...

UGGHH...

I'M OKAY. I'M NOT...
I DON'T... FEEL A THING.
HALLELUJAH!

PRAISE THE LORD!
GIVE ME... ANOTHER SNAKE.
YOU GOTTA BE FILLED WITH THE HOLY GHOST TO TAKE UP THE SERPENT. IF YOU AIN'T, THE SERPENT'LL LET YOU KNOW.

THE SERPENT'LL KEEP YOU HONEST.

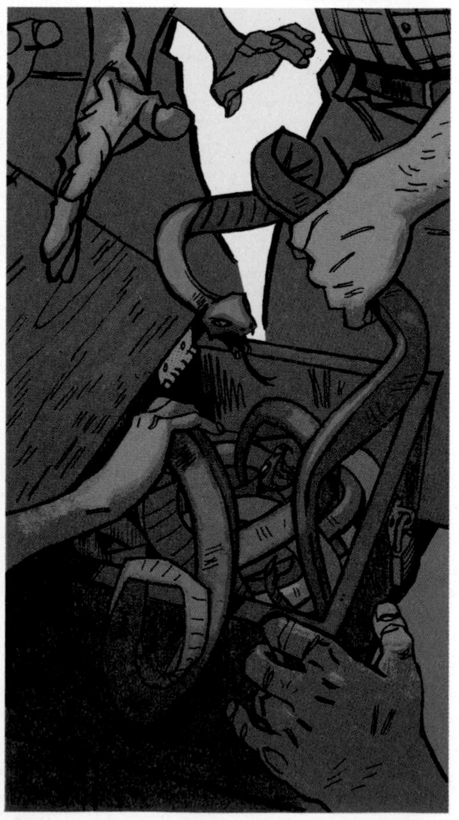

LOOK AT THAT. AIN'T THAT A SPREAD.
SQUIRREL DUMPLINGS. BOILED CRAWDADS. MAMMA RAY'S TURNIP GREENS. SQUASH CASSEROLE. GREEN BEAN CASSEROLE. SWEET POTATO CASSEROLE.
BOY, I TELL YA, WE GONE HAVE US A GOOD FELLOWSHIP TODAY, AIN'T WE?

OH MY. LOOKS LIKE **DEACON BOONE** EVEN BRUNG US SOME A' HIS FAMOUS FRESH SMOKED VENISON.
PRAISE THE LORD, BROTHER.

YOU BEST MAKE SURE YOU TRY SOME OF THAT PEACH COBBLER I BROUGHT, BROTHER DEACON. I KNOW IT'S YOUR FAVORITE.

MAKE SURE YOU SAVE ROOM FOR SOME OF MY BUTTER CAKE, DEACON. I MADE IT SPECIAL JUST FOR YOU.

ALL RIGHT NOW, BEFORE WE ENJOY THIS HERE FEAST, LET'S ALL JOIN HANDS AND SAY THE BLESSIN'.

DEAR LORD, WE THANK YOU FOR YOUR MANY BLESSINGS, LORD.
WE THANK YOU FOR THIS FOOD WE ARE ABOUT TO RECEIVE. AND FOR THE GIFTS OF THE SPIRIT WE HAVE ENJOYED IN YOUR NAME.

WATCH OVER US LORD, AND CONTINUE TO SHOW US YOUR WILL.
BE WITH ALL THOSE WHO COULDN'T BE HERE TODAY. THE SICK AND THE INFIRMED.
BE WITH DEACON POLK'S WIFE, LORD, AND HEAL HER OF HER RHEUMATISM.

AND BE WITH THE PARNELL FAMILY, LORD, AS THEY DEAL WITH THE GREAT INJUSTICE THAT HAS BEEN DONE TO THEIR DAUGHTER.
THEIR POOR, SWEET, SIMPLE-MINDED DAUGHTER.

MAY YOU BRING JUSTICE TO HER ATTACKER, LORD GOD, WHOEVER HE MAY BE.

THESE THINGS WE PRAY, LORD, IN THE NAME OF THY PRECIOUS SON, JESUS...
AMEN.

THE PARNELL GIRL WAS 23 YEARS OLD.
WITH THE BRAIN OF ABOUT A FIVE-YEAR-OLD.

HER MOMMA FOUND HER IN THE WOODS WITH HER CLOTHES TORN OFF AND BLOOD ALL OVER HER THIGHS.
SHE COULDN'T TELL NOBODY WHAT HAD HAPPENED OR WHO'D DONE IT.

BUT THE "WHAT" WAS FAIRLY OBVIOUS.
AND THE "WHO"...
TOOK A WHOLE 45 MINUTES TO FIGURE OUT.
MONROE

TOOK ME A LOT LESS TIME THAN THAT TO DECIDE WHAT TO DO ABOUT IT.

NOT TONIGHT.

TONIGHT I AIN'T HUNTIN' NO DEER.

HA HA HA HAAA HAA!
YEAH, KEEP THE FUCKING BEER COLD, ASSHOLE.
I'M ON MY FUCKING WAY.

FUCK NO, I AIN'T STAYING IN PINEY WOODS THIS WEEK. YOU THINK I'M GONNA MISS ALL THEM HOMECOMING PARTIES?
DALE ARLEY. WORKS AT A SAWMILL IN COTTON SPRINGS. LIVES WITH HIS GRANDPA IN PINEY WOODS.

LIKES TO GET DRUNK AND BRAG ABOUT RAPING RETARDED GIRLS.
SHIT. SOUNDS LIKE I GOT A FUCKING FLAT. I'LL CALL YA BACK.
SAVE ME SOME FUCKING BEER OR I'LL BEAT YOUR ASS.
FWAP
FWAP
FWAP

DALE WAS HEADED INTO TOWN. EVERY-BODY KNEW THAT.

APPARENTLY IT'S SOMETHIN' CALLED "HOMECOMING WEEK."
AW FUCK. FUCK YOU, TIRE. WHY YOU WANNA GO AND BLOW ON A NIGHT LIKE FUCKING...

OH SHIT.
TSSSSSHHHHHH
BUT DALE ARLEY AIN'T GONNA MAKE IT HOME.

I WAIT UNTIL HE TURNS.
UNTIL HE SEES ME.
OH FUCK.
I... I...

I WANT HIM TO SEE ME.

I WANT HIM TO KNOW WHY.

HEY, WELL LOOK WHO THE FUCK IT IS!
HOWDY, BOONE. GREAT DAY TO BE ON THE RIVER, AIN'T IT?
YOU NEED TO MOVE ALONG.

AND TELL THEM GIRLS TO PUT SOME CLOTHES ON. THERE'S FAMILIES LIVE ON THIS RIVER.
HEH. YOU OWN THE FUCKING RIVER NOW OR SOME-THING?

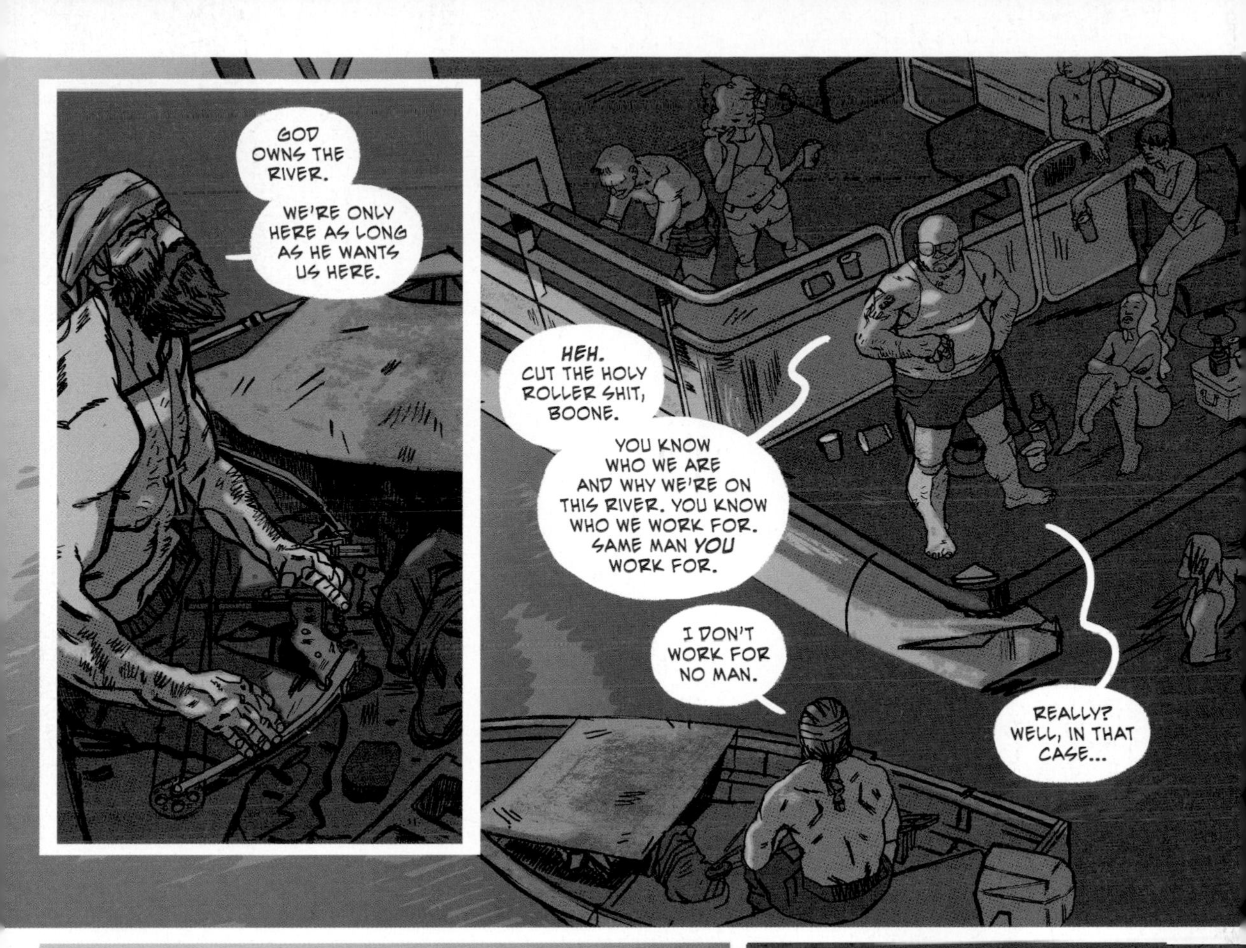
GOD OWNS THE RIVER.
WE'RE ONLY HERE AS LONG AS HE WANTS US HERE.
HEH. CUT THE HOLY ROLLER SHIT, BOONE.
YOU KNOW WHO WE ARE AND WHY WE'RE ON THIS RIVER. YOU KNOW WHO WE WORK FOR. SAME MAN *YOU* WORK FOR.
I DON'T WORK FOR NO MAN.
REALLY? WELL, IN THAT CASE...

BIG SHIPMENT THIS WEEK. BUT I RECKON THE BOYS UPRIVER WOULDN'T MIND IF SOME OF 'EM SHOWED UP SLIGHTLY USED.
WHY DON'T YOU TELL ME AGAIN WHOSE RIVER THIS IS, MOTHER-FUCKER?

MOVE ALONG, BOY.
OR WE'LL FIND OUT TOGETHER.

HEH. YOU JUST AIN'T NO DAMN FUN AT ALL, ARE YA, BOONE?
WE'LL TELL COACH YOU SAID HI.
RUN 'EM, REBS!

MOST TIMES BEING A LEADER IS ABOUT MAKING TOUGH CHOICES. STANDING STRONG NO MATTER WHAT. REMINDING FOLKS THERE'S LINES THAT CAN'T NEVER BE CROSSED.
BUT OTHER TIMES...
OTHER TIMES IT'S ABOUT MAKING COMPROMISES.

AND SOMETIMES, YOU CAN'T TELL THE DAMN DIFFERENCE NO MORE.
MAY ALL BE JUDGED BY THEIR DEEDS, HEAVENLY FATHER.
THY WILL BE DONE IN ALL THINGS.

SHANDALAH DO ANNA DOOLU MOOLLA!
MOOLA MALLA SHAMABALLA DOOLA!
HALLELUJAH! PRAISE THE LORD!
THE BIBLE TEACHES US THAT THE DEVIL CAME INTO EDEN IN THE GUISE OF A SERPENT. AND FOR A TIME, MAN LIVED SIDE BY SIDE WITH THE SERPENT.

they shall speak with new tongues;
they shall take up serpen
MAYBE HE HAD TO.
MAYBE HE HAD TO MAKE A DEAL WITH THE SERPENT TO PROTECT WHAT HE LOVED. TO KEEP PARADISE SAFE.
BUT A SERPENT IS STILL A SERPENT, NO MATTER THE DEAL.
AND AT SOME POINT, IT'S GONNA DO WHAT'S IN ITS NATURE.

..they shall cast out devils;
thing, shall
them;
YOU LIE WITH SERPENTS LONG ENOUGH, YOU WILL GET BIT.
HALLELUJAH, BROTHER!
I BEEN BIT MORE TIMES THAN I CAN REMEMBER.
AT WHAT POINT IS IT TIME TO BITE BACK?
I NEED AN ANSWER.
AND I DON'T BELIEVE I CAN WAIT NO LONGER TO GET IT.
I RECKON THERE'S JUST TOO MUCH COUNTRY IN ME, LORD.
BROTHER BOONE...?

I NEED TO KNOW IF NOW'S THE TIME WHEN I CAN SET THESE GOOD PEOPLE FREE.
WHEN I CAN RUN THAT SNAKE ON OUTTA EDEN FOR GOOD.
WHEN I CAN FINALLY KILL COACH BOSS.

Chapter 12

Vegetables

AIN'T NO BETTER FEELIN' THAN A WIN.

AAGHHH
WINNIN' MAKES YA FORGET ALL ABOUT BUSTED KNEES AN' BLACKOUT HEADACHES.
IT'LL TURN A GREY SKY BLUE--

IT'LL HEAL THE SICK AND TEACH THE BLIND TA SEE.
NNN... GGGGHHH...
SS-STOP... P-PLEASE...
TAKE THE LOWLIEST DOG AN' MAKE 'EM KING FOR A DAY.

YEAH. COME TA THINK OF IT--
REALLY AIN'T NOTHIN' WINNING CAIN'T FIX.
BLURGHGH!

GODDAMN IT, MATERHEAD.
ALL THEM SKANK CHERRIES YOU DONE POPPED, YOU'D THINK YOU'D BE USED TO A LITTLE BLOOD.

CLEAN THAT SHIT OFF YOUR FUCKIN' CHIN, WILL YA?
YOU WANT THE BOYS TO SEE YOU LOOKIN' LIKE A STRAIGHT-UP BITCH?

SSSNIFFFFF
WE GOT A GODDAMN EXAMPLE TO SET, MATER.

THERE'S MY LITTLE STONE-EYED KILLERS!

I SWEAR-- Y'ALL SO FUCKIN' BAD ASS I MUST BE Y'ALL'S REAL DADDY!

MY NAME'S EUGENE MAPLES. FOLKS CALL ME "MATERHEAD".
GOOD GODDAMN WORK, FELLAS.
FIRST ROUND'S ON MATER.
FULLBACK, 1993 STATE CHAMPION CRAW COUNTY RUNNIN' REBS.
THAT'S RIGHT--

SOUTHERN BASTARDS
I'M A WINNER.

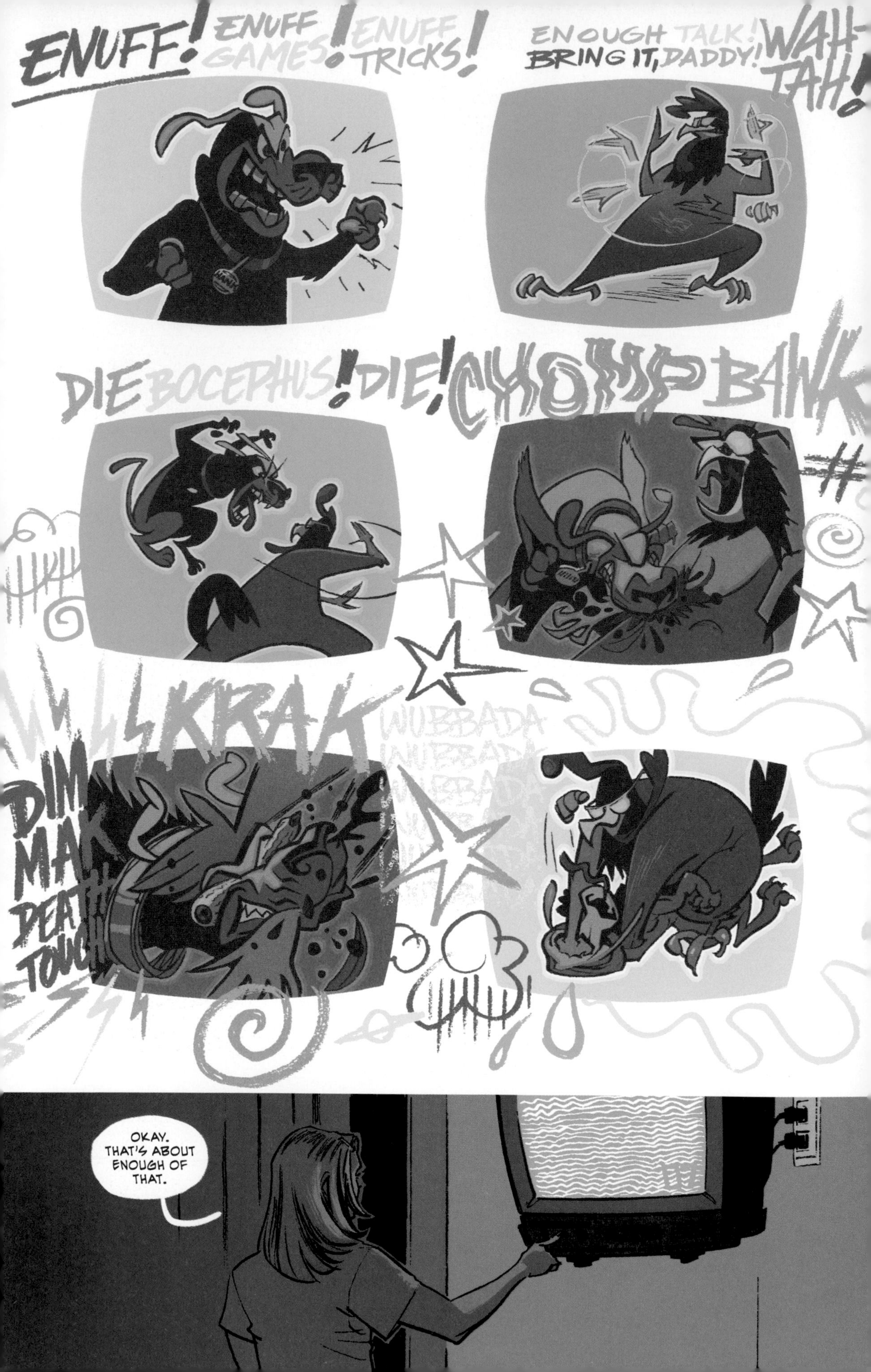
ENUFF! ENUFF GAMES! ENUFF TRICKS!
ENOUGH TALK! BRING IT, DADDY!
WAH-TAH!
DIE BOCEPHUS! DIE!
CHOMP
BANK
KRAK
WUBBADA WUBBADA
DIM MAK DEATH TOUCH
OKAY. THAT'S ABOUT ENOUGH OF THAT.

--IT'S WEDNESDAAAAAY NIGHT WAAAAAR ZOOONE!
SORRY, I KNOW YOU LOVE THEM CARTOONS, TAD--
BUT IF I SIT THROUGH ONE MORE I'M GONNA HAVE A CONNIPTION FIT.

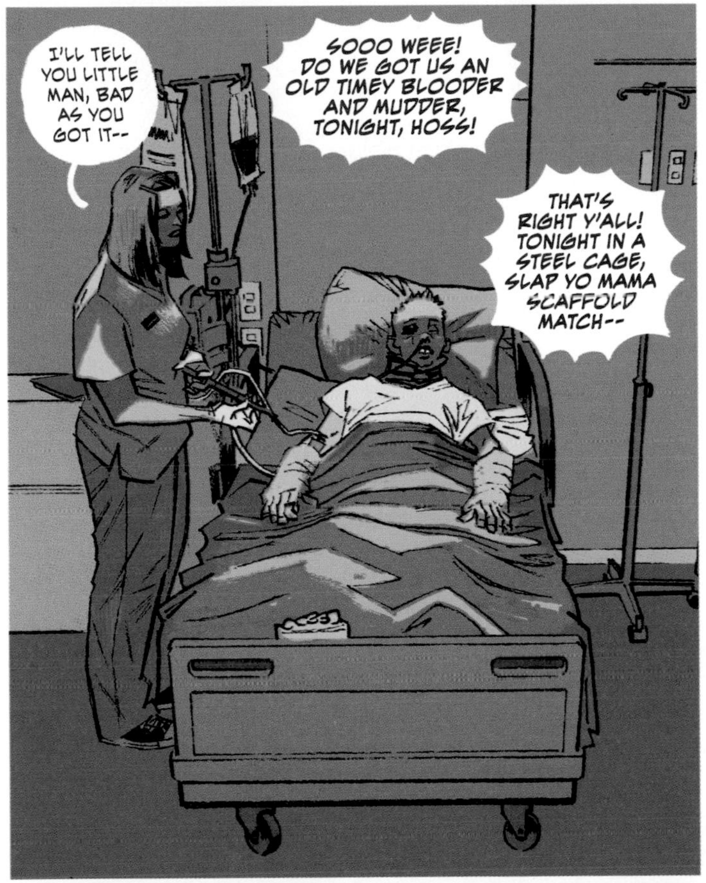
I'LL TELL YOU LITTLE MAN, BAD AS YOU GOT IT--
SOOO WEEE! DO WE GOT US AN OLD TIMEY BLOODER AND MUDDER, TONIGHT, HOSS!
THAT'S RIGHT Y'ALL! TONIGHT IN A STEEL CAGE, SLAP YO MAMA SCAFFOLD MATCH--

I'D TRADE PLACES WITH YOU IN A HEART-BEAT TO SLEEP LIKE THAT.
IT'S JOHNNY "BENCHPRESS" BARTELL VERSUS CHARGIN' CHACHO CAMARO--

THAT'S RIGHT! TONIGHT EVERYTHING'S ON THE LINE, Y'ALL!

BOSS
BBQ
IT'S HIM, ESAW.
IT'S JUST GOTTA BE.

WHOA BOY, BARTELL'S IN BIG TROUBLE NOW, JIM!
CAMARO'S GONNA I-ROC HIM TO SLEEP!

Ice Cream
I DIDN'T WANT TO BELIEVE IT BUT I SEEN HIM AGAIN LAST NIGHT.
SEEN HIM THAT NIGHT AT THE *TUBB HOUSE* WHEN WE MESSED THAT LEDBETTER BOY UP TOO.
OH NAW! OH NAW!
HOW YOU GONNA LET A FUCKIN' MEXICAN CHOKE YOU OUT, YOU FUCKIN' PUSSY!?

WARZONE
WHAT!? NO! WHAT IN!? WHAT IN ALL THE FUCK!?
THAT'S IT FOLKS! PUT JOHNNY IN A BODY BAG!
PUSSY WAGON TRAIN
I SEEN HIM EVERY NIGHT SINCE BIG DIED.
I WOKE UP THIS MORNING IN A POOL OF SWEAT AN' PISS.

I'M TELLIN' YOU, 'SAW--
THAT SHITTIN' DOG IS AFTER ME.
WAIT. DID YOU SAY YOU PISSED YOURSELF?
WHAT IN FUCK ARE YOU ON ABOUT, MATERHEAD?
THAT DOG, MAN. THE ONE THAT WAS FOLLOWIN' TUBB--
I'M TELLIN' YOU, IT'S ALWAYS AROUND. EVERY SINGLE TIME SOMETHIN' GOES WRONG IT--

MATER--I'VE HAD ENOUGH SUPERSTITIOUS VOODOO SHIT THIS WEEK TO LAST MY WHOLE FUCKIN' LIFE.
AIN'T NOTHING GONE WRONG, 'CEPT YOU PISSING YOURSELF LIKE A FUCKIN' KINDERGARTENER.
IT'S GODDAMN HOMECOMING, AND WE'RE GONNA LINE UP AND KICK WETUMPKA IN THE DICK.

LIKE ALWAYS.
BUT THIS-- THIS AIN'T JUST SOME STRAY DOG, 'SAW...
I THINK IT'S "REBEL".

REBEL!? *HA!* IF THAT MUTT WERE ALIVE IT'D BE SO OLD IT'D SHIT FOSSILS!
BESIDES, COACH HAD YOU PUT THAT FLEABAG DOWN AFTER--
AFTER IT BIT HIM TAKIN' THE FIELD AGAINST--

WETUMPKA, 'SAW.
BIT HIM LAST TIME WE LOST TO WETUMPKA.

JESUS FUCKIN' FUCK.

GODDAMN IT.

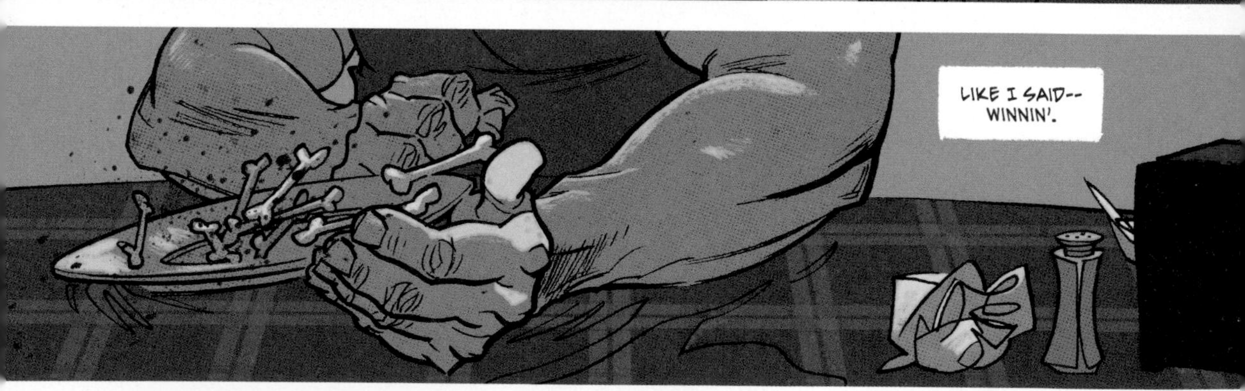

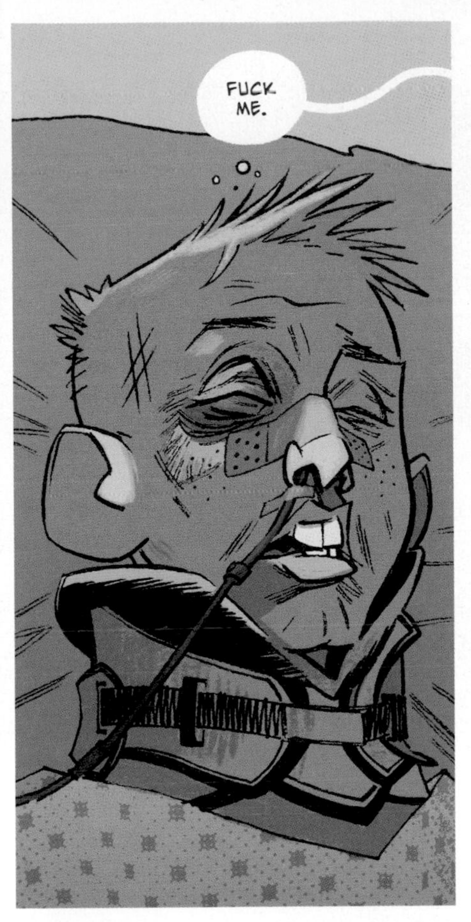
FUCK ME.

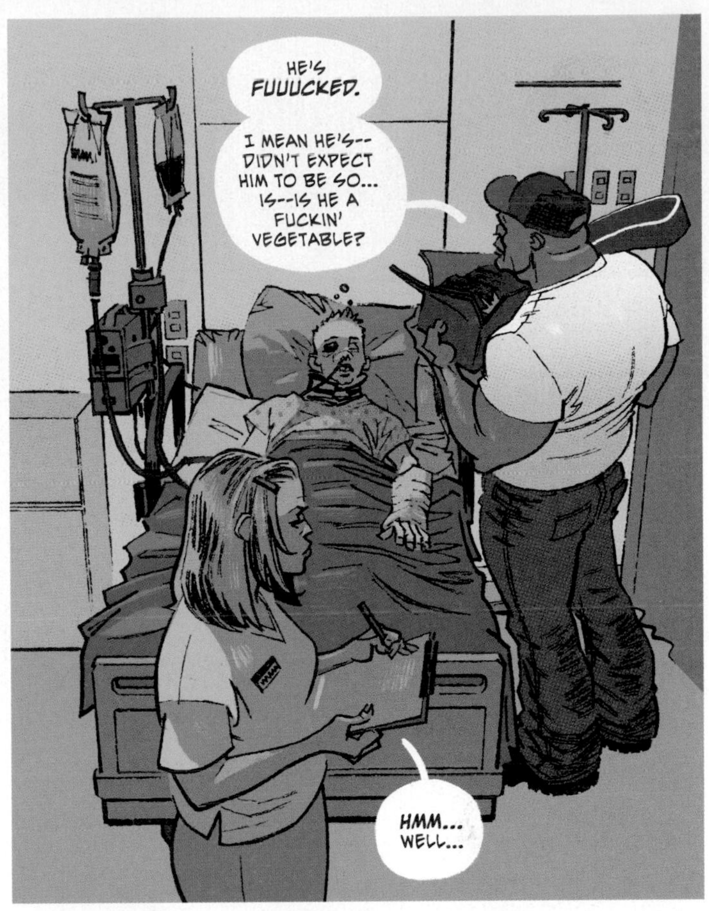
HE'S FUUUCKED.
I MEAN HE'S-- DIDN'T EXPECT HIM TO BE SO... IS--IS HE A FUCKIN' VEGETABLE?
HMM... WELL...

Broken left and right femur.
Shattered right fibula.
Broken ribs (6).
Broken left ulna.
Shattered right radial.
Hairline Parietal fracture.
Edema of the brain.
Bruised lung
Bruised Spleen.
Lacerated kidney
MUTE
HE NEEDS SLEEP TO HEAL AND DOPE TO SLEEP.
BUT HE'S STILL ALIVE IF YOU WANNA CALL IT THAT.
I DUNNO. ADD ENOUGH WATER AND SUNSHINE AND AIR--AND BEST CASE SCENARIO...

MAYBE HE'S A POTTED PLANT.

HEY...UH... HEY THERE, LITTLE FELLA.
HOW... HOW'S IT... UH...HOW'S IT GOIN'?

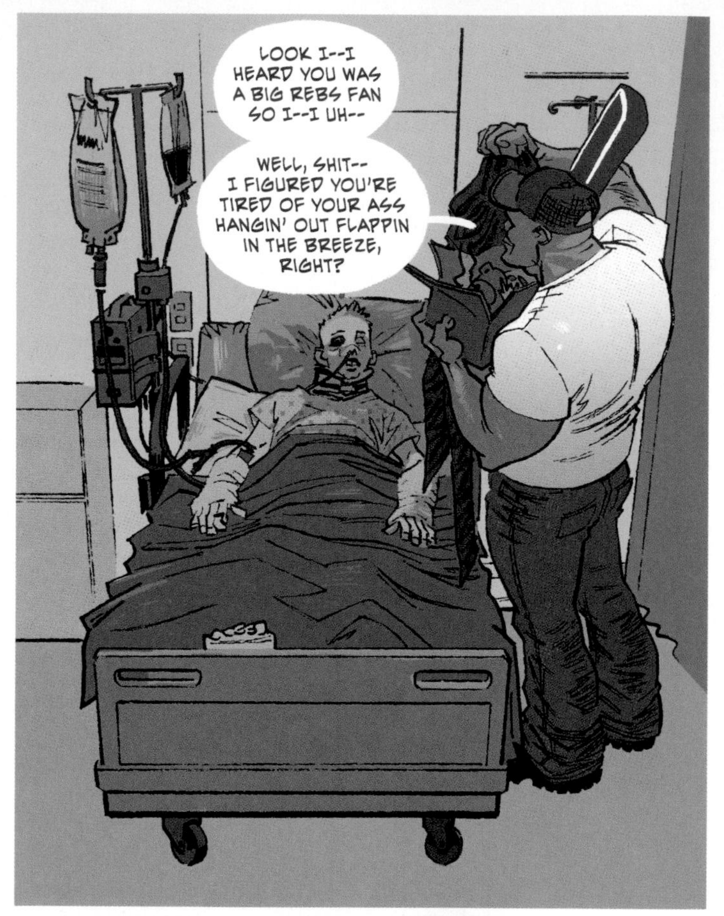
LOOK I--I HEARD YOU WAS A BIG REBS FAN SO I--I UH--
WELL, SHIT-- I FIGURED YOU'RE TIRED OF YOUR ASS HANGIN' OUT FLAPPIN IN THE BREEZE, RIGHT?

AND UH-- YEAH I GOT YOU SOME SWEET-ASS ZUBAZ AND THIS--
THIS HERE HAT.
YEAH. WE ONLY GIVE 'EM OUT TO THE COACHIN' STAFF. I CAIN'T NEVER FIND ONE TO FIT THIS MELLON I GOT SO...

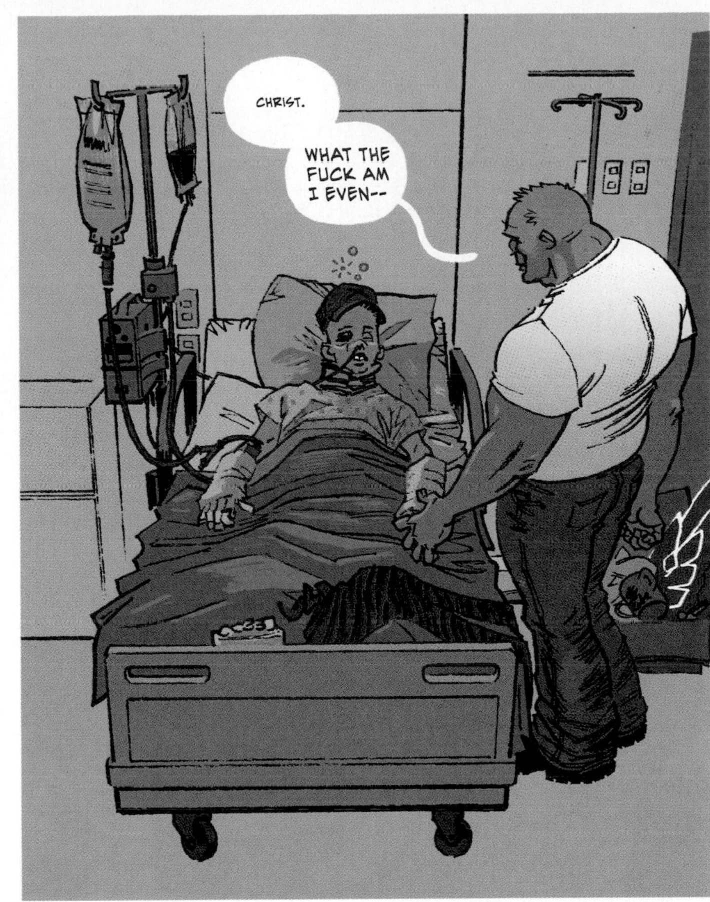
CHRIST.
WHAT THE FUCK AM I EVEN--

LOOK, I AIN'T--I AIN'T FUCKIN' SORRY OKAY?

NOT...NOT ABOUT WHAT HAPPENED TO YOUR FRIEND.

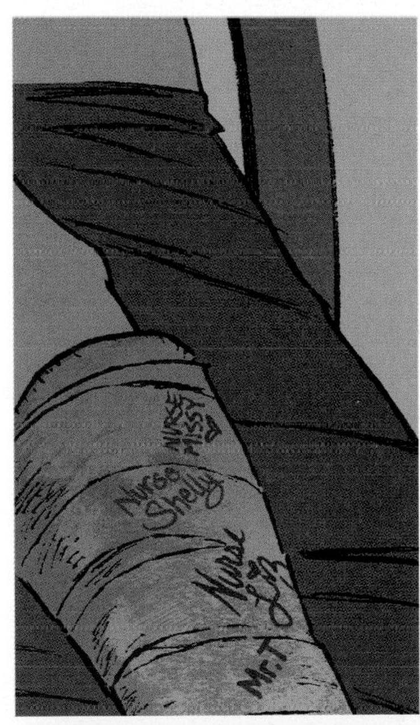
Nurse Missy
Nurse Shelly
Nurse Liz
Mr. T

TUBB WAS AN ASSHOLE. HE SHOULDN'T OF POKED THE FUCKIN' BEAR.

BUT HOW HOW--IT HAPPENED... WELL I...

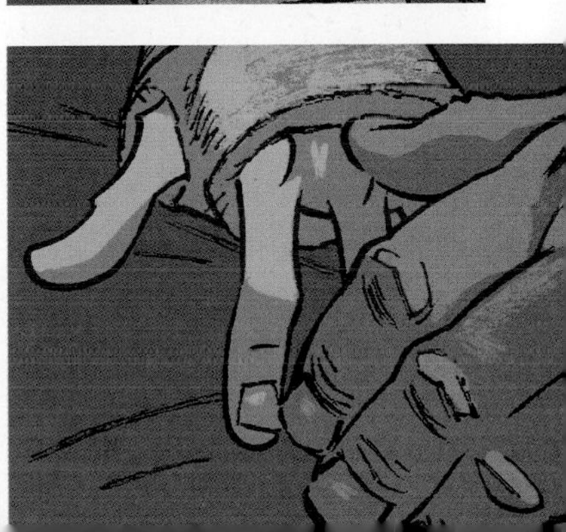

LOOK JUS'...I'LL MAKE YOU A DEAL, AIGHT?
SOON AS YOU'RE UP WALKIN' I'LL LET YOU STAND ON THE SIDELINES. EVERY SINGLE GAME.
HELL, I'LL EVEN LET YA CALL A PLAY OR TWO IN. WHO'S THAT GONNA HURT...

IT'S ALL SPINNIN' OUTTA CONTROL. AN' SOMEBODY'S GOTTA DO...SOMETHIN' TA TURN IT AROUND.
JUST...JUST HELP ME MAKE EVERYTHING ALL RIGHT.

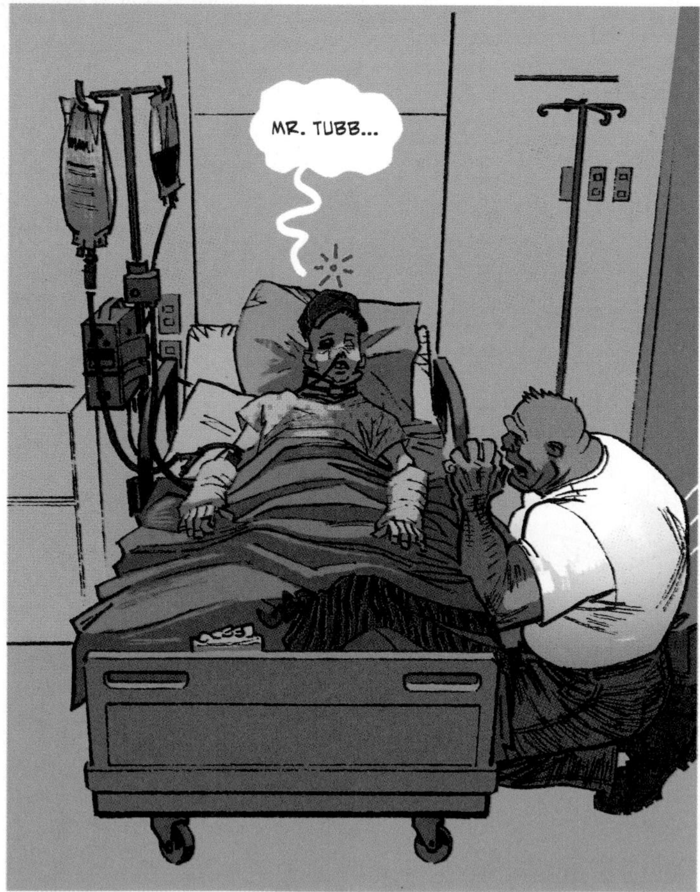
MR. TUBB...

WHAT DID YOU SAY HAPPENED TO MR. TUBB?

RRRRGGH!
RRRGGHH!
AH SAY, AH SAY--

AH SAY IT WITH **MAH FISTS!**

SQUOITE
YOU...
YOU...
YOU...AIN'T SUPPOSED TO BE HERE...

AIN'T YOUR TREE. AIN'T YOUR HOUSE.
WHERE'S MR. TUBB?

EARL TUBB A GOD DAMN MAN.
MR. TUBB AIN'T HERE NO MORE.
HE'S DEAD.

FUNNY. I WAS THINKING THE SAME THING.
MIND GETTIN' DOWN OUT OF THAT TREE?
LIBERTY
1996 S
EARL TUBB A GOD DAMN MAN.

NO. THIS... THIS AIN'T RIGHT...
IT'S ALL MIXED UP.
MR. TUBB CAIN'T BE DEAD.

SURE HE CAN.

RAH!
WHEN YOU MESS WITH THE BULL--
YOU GET THE HORNS.
YAH
SNIKT
Kiii
boosh!
HA!
GOODBYE EARL AINT IT DARK

COACH BOSS

YOU THOUGHT THAT OLD TREE WAS BIG AND TOUGH, HUH?
IMAGINE TRYIN' TO CHOP **HIM** DOWN.
IT WAS MY FAULT!
I WEREN'T THERE TA HELP HIM.
BRING HIM BACK! TAKE *ME* INSTEAD!

AND NOW WHY WOULD I WANT A PISSANT LITTLE TADPOLE LIKE YOU?
NAW. SORRY, BOY. THAT'S FAR TOO BIG A FISH TO THROW BACK.
YOU'LL HAVE TO DO BETTER.

COACH BOSS.
I CAN BRING YOU COACH BOSS.
CRUNCH
CRUNCH

HMMMM....
I DON'T KNOW, BOY. I JUST DON'T KNOW...
WHAT DO YOU THINK, OLD HANK? WOULD YOU A'DONE IT THIS A WAY?
HANK

TAP
TAP
TAP
TAP
R
FIELD HOUSE
COACH? COACH BOSS YOU IN THERE?

COACH-- I--I BEEN GOIN' OVER THE NEW GAME PLAN. AN' I JUST WANTED TO--AH--
WELL I THINK IT-- UH--
BOSS

IT--UH-- YEAH--IT LOOKS PRETTY GOOD I THINK...
I MEAN I GUESS...

SHIT. I JUST-- I JUST WANTCHA TO KNOW.
I'M DOIN' ALL I CAN, COACH.
I DONE ALL I CAN TO HELP.

DOUBLE YOU! AYE! OW! WIDE ASS OPEN, BOYS!
THAT'S HOW WE PRACTICE! THAT'S HOW WE PLAY!
THAT'S HOW WE LIVE EVERY DAMN DAY!
WHAT *THE FUCK* ARE YOU DOIN', MATER?
TRYIN' TO CONVINCE COACH TO CIRCLE JERK AROUND A DEAD GOAT OR SOME OTHER SCARED OLD WOMAN SHIT?
YOU SEE THAT? HOW *FIRED UP* THEM BOYS ARE?
THAT'S THE ONLY *BELIEF* WE NEED TO WIN THIS GAME.
YOU'RE POSITIVE, HUH?
YOU'RE GODDAMN RIGHT I AM.
YEAH. ME TOO.
POSITIVE YOU'RE A FUCKIN' DUMBASS.
DAY HE HIRED ME, COACH BOSS SAT ME DOWN TA EXPLAIN WHY--

AND IT WEREN'T CAUSE I WAS NO FOOTBALL GENIUS.
THAT'S RIGHT REBS, IT'S THE NIGHT YOU'VE ALL BEEN WAITING FOR!

HELL, I WEREN'T EVEN THAT GREAT A PLAYER.
TONIGHT! THE RIVALRY IS ONCE MORE RENEWED IN BLOOD!
HRRNNNH... HRRNNNH...

THAT'S RIGHT! TONIGHT UNDER THE BIG LIGHTS!
IT'S THE UNBEATEN WARRIORS OF WETUMPKA COUNTY--
C'MON... HRRNNNH... MOVE...

VERSUS THE LEGENDARY COACH EULESS BOSS--
BCAWK
AND YOUR UNDEFEATED CRAW COUNTY RUNNIN' REBS!
SAID IT WAS MY LOYALTY THAT HE VALUED.

SO STRAP IN, Y'ALL! HOMECOMING IS FINALLY--
THAT HE WAS READY TO RETURN.
click

SAID THERE WAS ALWAYS A PLACE FOR A MAN WHO PUT THE TEAM FIRST.

RRRRRRR
"MATER...,"
HE SAID--

"WHAT KEEPS A FOOTBALL TEAM ALIVE IS FINDIN' THE RIGHT PLAYERS."

"THEY AIN'T ALWAYS THE FASTEST, OR THE STRONGEST OR THE SMARTEST--"

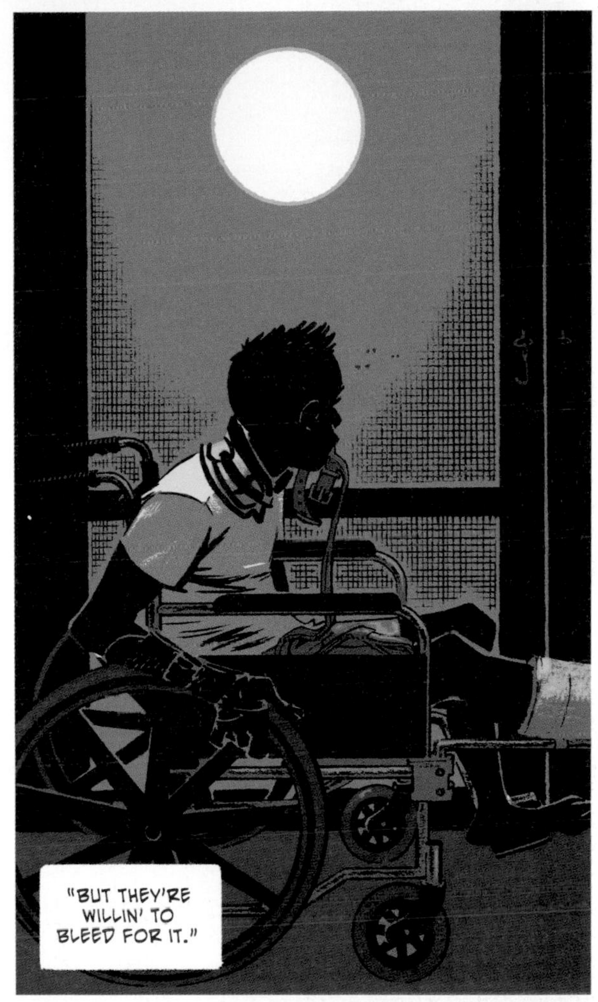
"BUT THEY'RE WILLIN' TO BLEED FOR IT."

A GOOD PLAYER IS A SOLDIER.
AND WITH ENOUGH SOLDIERS--

WHAT YOU'VE GOT IS AN ARMY.

Chapter 13

Fourth and Goal

BLEED IF YOU GOT TO!
BREAK YOUR FUCKING BONES IF THAT'S WHAT IT TAKES!
BUT DO NOT GIVE THESE MOTHER FUCKERS ANOTHER. GODDAMN. INCH!
I DON'T ASK NOTHIN' OF MY PLAYERS I DIDN'T ASK OF MYSELF WHEN I WAS THEIR AGE.
PLAY THIS PLAY LIKE YOUR WHOLE FUCKIN' LIFE DEPENDS ON IT!

IT'S FOURTH AND GOAL FROM THE THREE YARD LINE, AND IT LOOKS LIKE WETUMPKA'S GONNA GO FOR IT.
I'M SAYIN' PLAY ACTION.

IS THAT A RUNNIN' BACK? HE'S BIGGER THAN OUR DAMN LINEMEN.
BIGGEST KICK IN THE NUTS YOU CAN GET AS A DEFENSE AIN'T THE OTHER TEAM GETTIN' BEHIND YOUR SAFETIES FOR A BIG BOMB OR OUT-FINESSIN' YA WITH SOME FANCY TRICKERATION BULLSHIT.

IT'S WHEN THEY LOOK YA SQUARE IN THE EYE...
AND YOU KNOW THEY'RE GONNA RUN THE BALL RIGHT AT YA.
PLAYERS KNOW IT. COACHES KNOW IT.
EVERY ASSHOLE IN THE STANDS KNOWS IT.
STUFF 'EM, REBS!
HIT 'EM IN THE FUCKIN' MOUTH!

PLAY ACTION AND THEY'LL LOOK FOR THE TIGHT END IN THE BACK OF THE ENDZONE.
THEY AIN'T GOT THE BALLS TO TRY AND RUN IT ON US HERE.
DO THEY?
SELL-OUT TO STOP THE RUN. SIGNAL IT IN.
HOLY SHIT.

HUT HUT HIKE!
YOU KNOW EXACTLY WHAT'S COMING...

KICK THEIR INJUN ASSES!

AND YOU STILL CAN'T STOP IT.

TOUCHDOWN,
WETUMPKA
COUNTY.

THERE'S LOSIN' AND THEN THERE'S GETTIN' BEAT. EVEN I LOSE EVERY NOW AND THEN.
HIT SOMEBODY, YOU FAGGOTS!
IT'S ALL RIGHT, BOYS! YOU JUST DO YOUR BEST OUT THERE!
SON OF A FUCKIN' BITCH!
CLAP CLAP CLAP
FUCK YOU, BRENDA!

BUT I AIN'T BEEN BEAT SINCE I WAS A BOY.
WHAT THE FUCK WAS THAT? THIS AIN'T FLAG FOOTBALL! YOU'RE SUPPOSED TO TACKLE THE MOTHERFUCKER!
PULL YOUR HEADS OUT YOUR PUSSIES AND LET'S PLAY LIKE FUCKIN' REBS!

SINCE BEFORE I PUT A BULLET IN MY DADDY'S BRAIN.

SOUTHERN BASTARDS

HE WAS TIRED. I SHOULDA SEEN THAT.

HE WAS OLD AS HELL. PROBABLY KNEW HE WASN'T GONNA BE ABLE TO KEEP GOIN' FOR TOO MUCH LONGER.
AND HE DIDN'T NEVER WANNA BE NO BURDEN TO NOBODY. DIDN'T WANNA WIND UP LAYIN' IN HIS OWN SHIT IN SOME SORRY ASS NURSIN' HOME.
THAT MUST BE WHY.
WHY BIG BLOWED HIS OWN GODDAMN BRAINS OUT.

I CAN RESPECT THAT.
I EVER GET TO THE POINT WHERE I CAN'T COACH 'EM NO MORE, I'LL DO THE SAME DAMN THING.
GRADE AA
UTTER
I JUST WISH HE'D HAVE FUCKIN' WAITED UNTIL NEXT DAMN WEEK.
BIG KNOWED WHAT'S AT STAKE, WHENEVER WE STEP ON THAT FIELD.
WE CAN'T AFFORD TO LET 'EM SEE US LOOK MORTAL. NOT IN A GAME LIKE THIS.
NOT IN CRAW COUNTY.

NOT WITH THE VULTURES WE GOT CIRCLING ALL AROUND US.
MAYOR BUTTERWORTH AIN'T HAPPY.

YOU'RE HIS WIFE, MISS LEDDY. AIN'T IT YOUR JOB TO KEEP HIS ASS HAPPY? SURE AS HELL AIN'T MINE.
DON'T YOU GO GETTIN' SMART WITH ME, EULESS BOSS. YOU GOT A LOT TO ANSWER FOR HERE AND YOU DAMN WELL KNOW IT.

WHAT I GOT IS A GAME TO GET READY FOR. DID YOU REALLY CALL ME DOWN HERE THE DAY BEFORE HOMECOMING FOR THIS--
SHHH!
WHAT IS IT, SWEETIE-BOO?

THE MAYOR WANTS TO KNOW HOW YOU PLAN ON WINNIN' TOMORROW WITHOUT YOUR PRIZE NIGGER.

DOES HE NOW? YOU SURE THAT'S WHAT HE SAID? WHY DON'T I LET HIM WHISPER IT TO ME?
I SWEAR, I'D THINK A MAN WHO'S FOULED UP AS MUCH AS YOU HAVE LATELY WOULD HAVE THE GOL-DARN DECENCY TO BE A BIT MORE SUPPLICANT WHEN HE'S CALLED INTO THIS OFFICE.
FIRST THAT MESS WITH BERT TUBB'S SON. NOW YOUR SECRET FOOTBALL RAIN MAN DONE ATE A BULLET AND LEFT YOU HIGH AND DRY.
YOU AIN'T OFF TO THE BEST START THIS SEASON, ARE YA, COACH?
AIN'T LOST A GAME. AIN'T ABOUT TO.

IT AIN'T JUST THE MAYOR WHO AIN'T HAPPY THOUGH, IS IT? THE COMPSON GAL FROM THE BANK COME TO SEE HIM THE OTHER DAY.
THAT IS ONE NERVOUS BLONDE. WITH A WHOOOLE LOTTA SECRETS LOCKED IN HER LITTLE VAULT. WHICH OUGHTTA MAKE YOU MIGHTY NERVOUS TOO.
FOLKS SAY YOUR SHERIFF DON'T SEEM NONE TOO HAPPY NEITHER. THE MAYOR HEARD YOU TWO EVEN WENT AT IT LIKE A COUPLA BANTY ROOSTERS THE OTHER DAY. HE SURE WISHES HE COULDA SEEN THAT.

AND NOW HE HEARS THAT EVEN YOUR OLD BUDDIES IN MOBILE ARE STARTIN' TO--
YOU SHOULD TELL THE MAYOR NOT TO BELIEVE EVERY GODDAMN BIT OF GOSSIP HE HEARS. ESPECIALLY IF HE WANTS TO KEEP ON BEIN' MAYOR.

YOU'RE SCARED. ONLY TIME YOU THREATEN HIM IS WHEN YOU'RE SCARED.
BUT THE MAYOR AIN'T SCARED OF YOU, EULESS. NEVER HAS BEEN.
YOU AIN'T NOTHIN' BUT A GLORIFIED P.E. COACH. WHO'S IN A WHOLE BIG MESS OF TROUBLE. THE MAYOR'D LIKE YOU TO REMEMBER THAT.
THE MAYOR KNOWS WHAT A DIRTY LITTLE BOY YOU REALLY ARE. AND WITHOUT HIM...WELL...
I THINK THE MAYOR JUST SHIT HIS FUCKIN' DIAPER. BEST GET THAT CHANGED, MISS LEDDY.

IF I WAS YOU, COACH... I WOULDN'T LOSE THIS GAME.

AND IF I WAS YOU, MA'AM, I'D PRAY HE DON'T DIE. OR EVER GET WELL ENOUGH TO TALK FOR HISSELF.

HE'S GONE. YOU CAN SHUT THE FUCK UP NOW, CLAUDE.

SCORE AT HALFTIME IS WARRIORS 20... REBS 3.
AND NOW LET'S GET READY FOR THE RUNNIN' REBS MARCHING BAND AND YOUR CRAW COUNTY HOMECOMING COURT...
WHO'S SHITTIN' THEIR PANTS NOW, ASSHOLE?

YOU GONE REMEMBER THIS DAY FOR THE REST OF YOUR LIVES.
NO MATTER WHAT HAPPENS IN THESE NEXT TWO QUARTERS.
AND IF YOU EVER TRY AND FORGET IT, WON'T NOBODY IN THIS COUNTY EVER LET YA.

I AIN'T GONNA SCREAM AND HOLLER AT Y'ALL. NOT TONIGHT. I AIN'T GONNA KICK NO LOCKERS OR RAISE NO HELL.
I'M JUST GONNA SIT HERE AND LET Y'ALL FIGURE OUT FOR YOUR-SELVES...
...WHAT SORTA **MAN** YOU WANNA BE.

THE KIND WHO'S FULLA **FIGHT.**
OR FULLA **QUIT.**

IF YOU WANNA QUIT...DO IT NOW.
THERE'S THE DOOR. WALK THE HELL ON OUTTA HERE. WON'T NOBODY TRY AND STOP YA. GO TELL YOUR MOMMAS YOU'RE READY TO GO HOME.

YOU WALK OUT THERE, YOU WON'T BE ALONE.
YOU'LL FIND PLENTY A' FOLKS IN THEM STANDS... WHO'RE JUST LIKE YA.

"FOLKS WHO CAN'T BE GREAT THEMSELVES."
"WHO ONLY FEED OFF THE GREATNESS OF OTHERS."
REB
HEH. BEST GAME I'VE SEEN IN A LONG ASS TIME.

"THEY'RE ALL WAITIN' ON YA."

REBS

"GO ON OUT THERE AND JOIN 'EM"
EVENING, MS. COMPSON. HOW'S YOUR SISTER DOING THESE--
NOT INTERESTED IS HOW SHE'S DOING.

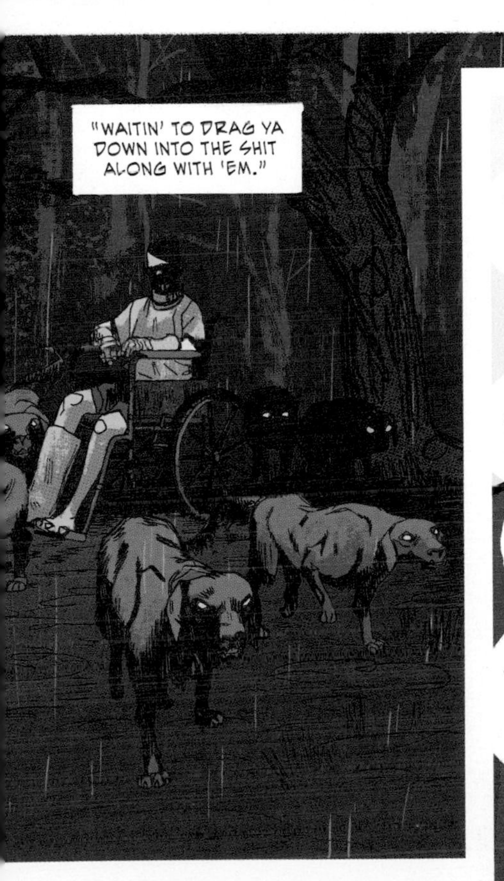
"WAITIN' TO DRAG YA DOWN INTO THE SHIT ALONG WITH 'EM."
IF YOU DON'T WALK OUT THAT DOOR...IF YOU DON'T WANNA QUIT...
THEN I'M GONE NEED YOU BOYS TO FIGHT.
FIGHT FOR EVERYTHING WE'VE EVER BUILT HERE.
FOR ALL THE BOYS WHO WORE THOSE HELMETS BEFORE YA. WHO BLED IN 'EM.
FOR ALL THEM TROPHIES Y'ALL WALK PAST IN THE HALLWAY THAT SAY WE'RE THE BEST THAT EVER WAS.
FOR COACH BIG.
I NEED YA TO GO OUT THERE AND FIGHT LIKE A PACK A' CRAZED FUCKIN' DOGS.
I NEED YA TO FIGHT LIKE REBS.
ANY OF YOU BOYS THINK YOU CAN DO THAT FOR ME?

DAMN. THAT WAS SURE SOME SPEECH, COACH. THEM BOYS ARE READY TO RUN THROUGH A BRICK WALL FOR YA NOW.
YEAH, ONLY IT AIN'T NO BRICK WALL WE GOT TO WORRY ABOUT, IS IT?
IT'S WETUMPKA'S FUCKIN' 800 POUND RUNNIN' BACK. THAT FAT ASS MOTHERFUCKER IS KILLIN' US.

COACH...
NEXT PLAY THAT KID GETS THE BALL, LET ME SEND A COUPLE BOYS DIVIN' AT HIS KNEES.
WE'LL GET HIS ASS OUTTA THAT GAME RIGHT QUICK.
RIGHT, COACH?
THAT'S YOUR SECOND HALF ADJUSTMENT, ESAW? THAT'S ALL YOU GOT FOR ME?
WELL... YEAH...I JUST THOUGHT...
AROUND HERE, WE WIN FOOTBALL GAMES BY PLAYIN' FOOTBALL. YOU SAYIN' I CAN'T **COACH** 'EM NO MORE? IS THAT WHAT YOU'RE SAYIN'?
NO, COACH, I'D...I'D NEVER...
BIG'S STILL GOT MORE BRAINS THAN YOU EVER DID. EVEN WITH HALF HIS BLOWED OUT THE BACK OF HIS SKULL.
MATERHEAD'S THE NEW DEFENSIVE COORDINATOR.
WHAT?!
WHAT!?!
WUMM
BET YOU'RE ***MISSIN'*** OLE' BIG RIGHT ABOUT NOW, AIN'T YA?
AH HELL.

NOT THAT IT WOULDA MATTERED EVEN IF HIS OLD BLIND ASS WAS HERE.
DON'T KNOW HOW Y'ALL DO IT IN WETUMPKA COUNTY, COACH, BUT AROUND HERE, WE PLAY ALL FOUR QUARTERS.
WARRIORS

OH BELIEVE ME, WE'LL BE PLAYIN' RIGHT 'TIL THE WHISTLE.
I WANNA ENJOY EVERY LAST DAMN SECOND OF THIS.
WE'LL SEE ABOUT THAT.

WHAT, DID YOU GO OUT AT HALFTIME AND RECRUIT YOURSELF A NEW TEAM OR SOMETHIN'?
SEE, THAT'S THE BEST THING ABOUT ALL THIS, AIN'T IT? WE AIN'T OUT-SCHEMIN' YA.
WE'RE OUT-HUSTLIN' YA. OUT HITTIN' YA. WE'RE JUST FLAT-OUT WHOOPIN' YA.
HEH. WE LOOK MORE LIKE A COACH BOSS TEAM THAN YOURS DOES.
HOW'S THAT FEEL, EULESS? GETTIN' BEAT AT YOUR OWN DAMN GAME?

EXIT
HOW'S IT FEEL BEING AN ASSHOLE, CHESTER?
GAME AIN'T OVER YET.
NO, IT WASN'T.
UNFORTUNATELY FOR US.

IN THE SECOND HALF, IT ONLY GOT **WORSE**.
OUR BOYS PLAYED AS HARD AS THEY COULD. FOR ABOUT 10 MINUTES OR SO. AFTER THAT...

YOU COULD SEE THE FIGHT GO OUT OF 'EM.
THEY JUST WANTED IT TO BE OVER. THEY JUST WANTED TO GO HOME.
I'D SEEN THAT LOOK BEFORE ON A FOOTBALL FIELD. MANY TIMES.

JUST NEVER IN THE EYES OF MY OWN TEAM.

RUNNIN' REBS
HOME
06:45
VISITOR
QTR
TOL
BALL ON
WHOOOO! I'M SURE GLAD BIG DIDN'T LIVE TO SEE THAT.
FUCK YOU, CHESTER. I HOPE YOUR KIDS GET ASS CANCER.
HA! SEE YA NEXT YEAR, EULESS. IF YOU'RE STILL HERE.
WARRIORS
HOME

I HOLD MY HEAD HIGH AS I LEAVE THE FIELD. AND LOOK ALL THEM VULTURES RIGHT IN THEIR BEADY LITTLE EYES.
I AIN'T DEAD YET, YOU SONS A BITCHES.

JUST A BIT BLOODY IS ALL. AND THAT'S ALL RIGHT.
I BEEN BLOODY BEFORE.

BIG CHIEF
CHOPPED BBQ
CHOP 'EM
WARRIORS
BIG CHIEF BBQ
HOLY SHIT, MAN, YOU RAN THROUGH THEM CRAW COUNTY BOYS LIKE THEY WAS *NOTHIN'.*

SHIT, THEY *WAS* NOTHIN'.
THE BIG FUCKIN' SCARY RUNNIN' REBS.
35
35

I DON'T KNOW WHAT PEOPLE WAS EVER SO FUCKIN' SCARED ABOUT. THEY WEREN'T NOTHIN' BUT A BUNCHA LITTLE--
YOU THINK YOU *TOUGH,* BIG BOY?

WHY DON'T YOU TRY RUNNIN' THROUGH *ME.*

BIG CHIEF
HOLY FUCK... THAT'S COACH BOSS.
WHY DON'T YOU TAKE YOUR DRUNK ASS BACK TO CRAW COUNTY, OLD MAN. BEFORE YOU GET HURT.
HE'S DRUNK AS FUCKIN' SHIT.
DAB ON 'EM

EITHER YOU RUN THROUGH ME, BOY. OR I'M GONNA GO THROUGH YOU.
YOU GOT FIVE SECONDS TO MAKE UP YOUR MIND.

DO IT.
LAY HIS OLD ASS OUT.
DAB ON 'EM
YOU CRAZY OLD MAN.
WILD TURKEY
DAB ON 'EM
HRRRGGN

HUGGH
DAB ON

DAB ON 'EM
UGGGHH.
WHUMP

DON'T NEVER FORGET THIS, BOY.
BUT IF YOU TELL ANYBODY THIS HAPPENED... MY WHOLE DAMN TEAM'LL BE RAPIN' YOUR MOMMA YOU HEAR ME?

WE'LL SEE YOU SONS A BITCHES IN THE PLAYOFFS.

LET THE VULTURES CIRCLE.
WARRIORS

LET 'EM COME, IF THEY GOT THE GUTS.
I'LL BE RIGHT FUCKIN' HERE.
FOR AS LONG AS I GODDAMN WANT.

Chapter 14

Boots on the Ground

IN *AFGHANISTAN,* I WAS PART OF A MARINE CORPS FEMALE ENGAGEMENT TEAM.
OUR JOB WAS TO INTERACT WITH THE LOCAL FEMALE POPULATION. TO GATHER INFORMATION AND IMPLEMENT COMMUNITY DEVELOPMENT PROGRAMS.
DISCOVER ALABAMA DINOSAURS
at McWane Science Center
Gate
A3
WE WERE OPERATING IN POOR, RURAL COMMUNITIES, AMONG A FIERCELY RELIGIOUS POPULACE.
PEOPLE WHO WERE DEEPLY MISTRUSTFUL OF OUTSIDERS. WHO PUT MORE FAITH IN RUMORS THAN THEY DID THE WORD OF THEIR OWN GOVERNMENT.
IN A LAND WITH A LONG HISTORY OF VIOLENCE.
IN OTHER WORDS...
I'D BEEN TRAINING FOR THAT JOB MY ENTIRE LIFE.

CALL ME THE SECOND YOU LAND.
OR BETTER YET, JUST TURN AROUND AND FLY RIGHT BACK.
IT TAKES TWO MILO'S CHEESEBURGERS, A SLICE OF COCONUT PIE FROM JOHNNY RAY'S AND A FEW BEERS FROM THE GARAGE CAFE...

BEFORE I'M ABLE TO WORK UP THE NERVE.
WHAT'S DONE IS DONE, ROBERTA. HE'S DEAD, AND THERE AIN'T NOTHING NOBODY CAN--

RRRR
RR

ARK!
ARK ARK ARK
ARK

DON'T REMEMBER HIM HAVING A DOG.

SOON AS I OPEN THE DOOR, IT HITS ME. THE SMELL OF STALE BEER AND SPOILT MILK AND AQUA VELVA AFTERSHAVE.
SMELLS LIKE A SAD OLD MAN.

SMELLS LIKE **EARL**.

TUBB

THIS AIN'T THE HOUSE I WAS BORN IN.
THIS IS WHERE MY DADDY MOVED AFTER HIM AND MY MOMMA SPLIT UP.
I COULDN'T TELL YOU HOW MUCH I EVER REALLY KNEW THE MAN WHO LIVED IN THIS HOUSE.
4 YEARS. SEPT
"Biscuit" - DANNY '72
- Khe Sanh -
August 1975
OR EXACTLY HOW MUCH I OWE HIM NOW THAT HE'S GONE.
OPEN UP! THIS IS THE POLICE!
KNNGK! KNNGK! KNNGK!

SOMETHING I CAN HELP YOU WITH, OFFICERS?
WE'VE HAD REPORTS OF A SUSPICIOUS CHARACTER IN THE NEIGHBORHOOD.
WE GONE NEED YOU TO STEP OUTSIDE WITH US, MA'AM.
IS THIS YOUR HOUSE?

I'VE HAD BOOTS ON THE GROUND IN BAMA FOR ABOUT THREE HOURS NOW AND IT ALREADY FEELS LIKE I'M AS CLOSE TO BEING SHOT AS I EVER WAS ON PATROL BACK IN KABUL.
BIRMINGHAM, ALA.
Magic City

ROLL FUCKING TIDE, I RECKON.

I REALLY HOPE YOU AIN'T DOING THIS JUST TO PISS ME OFF.

YOU'RE ONLY SAYING THAT 'CAUSE THAT'S WHAT YOU DID.
BUT I AIN'T YOU, DADDY. AND AFGHANISTAN AIN'T VIETNAM.
I HOPE TO HELL NOT.

'BERTA...
I HOPE YOU KNOW HOW...HOW MUCH I...
...THAT I AIN'T NEVER BEEN MUCH OF A DAMN...
...AND FOR ALL THEM TIMES I...HELL...

DADDY, SAVE IT FOR WHEN I'M OVER THERE. IT'LL GIVE US SOMETHING TO TALK ABOUT WHEN YOU CALL.

YOU KEEP YOURSELF HYDRATED. AND STAY IN THE REAR WITH THE GEAR AS MUCH AS YOU CAN.
DON'T GO THINKING YOU'RE RAMBO. THE RAMBOS TEND NOT TO MAKE IT BACK.
YEAH, BUT THE *TUBBS* DO.
GOODBYE, DADDY.

A DAMN WAR HERO. YOU BELIEVE THAT SHIT?
FUCKIN' OBAMA.
RRRRR
SPLUCH
GODDAMNIT.

Voicemail
572-0624
Charlotte, NC
at 4:59 PM
Speaker
Call Back
Delete
Dad
mobile
Dad
mobile
Dad
mobile
417-9150
Rock Hill, SC
I KNOW YOU'RE IN ALABAMA, ROBERTA. YOU'RE AT HIS HOUSE, AIN'T YA?
THERE'S NOTHING IN THAT HOUSE FOR YOU, GIRL. THERE NEVER WAS.

YOUR DADDY WASN'T HERE EVEN WHEN HE WAS ALIVE, WAS HE?

DON'T YOU GO CHASING HIM NOW THAT HE'S GONE.

HOT SHIT
CAYENNE PEPPER

DON'T YOU GO BEING A TUBB, ROBERTA. THAT'S JUST YOUR NAME. THAT AIN'T WHO YOU--
BLIP

WHAT THE HELL'D YOU DO TO MY DOG?

YOU MEAN THE DOG THAT DID ALL THIS TO MY DADDY'S PORCH?
YOUR *DADDY?*
SHIT. YOU'RE EARL'S DAUGHTER?
HELL, I RECKON I SHOULDN'T BE SURPRISED.

LET ME GUESS, YOU WERE A GOOD FRIEND OF HIS?
HEH, YOU DIDN'T KNOW YOUR DADDY SO GOOD, DID YA?
EARL DIDN'T HAVE TOO MANY FRIENDS. 'SPECIALLY NOT 'ROUND HERE.

SO THEN I GUESS YOU AIN'T HERE TO HELP ME CLEAN UP THIS MESS?
MY DOG'S BEEN COUGHING AND SNEEZING ALL DAMN MORNING. EYES ALL RED. SHIT ALL RUNNY.
SMELLS ALMOST LIKE HE GOT INTO A MESS OF **CAYENNE PEPPER.** NOW HOW YOU FIGURE THAT MIGHTA HAPPENED?

GOD KNOWS WHAT A DOG CAN GET INTO, WHEN IT DON'T KEEP TO ITS OWN YARD.

FUNNY. I WAS JUST THINKING THE SAME DAMN THING.

YOU AIN'T REALLY FIXIN' TO MOVE IN HERE, ARE YA?
'CAUSE A GIRL LIKE YOU'D PROBABLY LIKE IT BETTER OVER IN FORESTDALE OR BESSEMER.
SCHOOLS OUT THERE GOT REAL GOOD FOOTBALL TEAMS. HOW MANY KIDS YOU GOT? FOUR OR FIVE?

NEGATIVE, PRIVATE TUBB, YOU DO NOT HAVE PERMISSION TO ENGAGE. I REPEAT...
SO HOW ABOUT THAT CRIMSON TIDE, AM I RIGHT?

HEH. WE'RE AUBURN FANS, GIRL.
YEAH, SOMETHING TELLS ME, YOU GONE HAVE ABOUT AS MUCH LUCK MAKING FRIENDS AROUND HERE AS YOUR DADDY DID.
WAR DAMN EAGLE.

NEVER MIND THE DOG BEWARE OF OWNER!
HEARTS AND MINDS, PRIVATE. HEARTS AND MINDS.
HEY, LITTLE MAN. WHAT'S YOUR NAME?
I...
WILLIE!
WHAT THE HELL ARE YOU DOING?!
OW! I DIDN'T...
DON'T YOU BACK-TALK ME, BOY! GO TEAR A DAMN SWITCH OFF THE TREE!
AND IT BETTER BE A BIG ONE! I'M GONE TAN YOUR LITTLE HIDE!

THERE ARE TWO THINGS I KNOW GOOD AND DAMN WELL EARL TUBB NEVER CARED FOR.
LONG HAIR ON BOYS. AND AN OVERGROWN YARD.

THERE WERE MORE THAN TWO, OF COURSE. GOD, WERE THERE MORE. BUT THEM'S THE FIRST ONES THAT COME TO MIND.
NOW I CAN'T TAKE BACK ANY OF THE MULLETS OR AFROS I BRUNG HOME OVER THE YEARS, DADDY, BUT I RECKON I CAN MOW THE GRASS JUST ONE LAST...

WELL SHIT.
YOU'RE JUST THE GIFT THAT KEEPS ON GIVING, AIN'T YA, DADDY?
TURNS OUT I DIDN'T HAVE TO GO ALL THE WAY TO THE DESERT TO FIND ME A WAR.

EARL TUBB...
YOU'RE MY VIETNAM.

WHY ARE YOU DOING THIS TO ME?

HUMPF
WHY WON'T YOU CALL ME BACK, ROBERTA?
I CAN'T SLEEP 'CAUSE I'M WORRIED SICK ABOUT YOU. ABOUT WHAT KINDA TROUBLE YOU'RE GONNA GET YOURSELF INTO.

AND FOR WHAT? YOU DON'T OWE NOTHING TO THAT MAN. NONE OF US DO.
THUMP!

EARL TUBB MADE HIS OWN DAMN BED. NOW LET HIM LIE IN IT.
YOUR FATHER'S DEAD, ROBERTA, BUT YOU STILL HAVE A MOTHER. AND YOUR MOTHER SAYS CALL ME BACK WHEN YOU GET--

YOU MUSTA LOST YOUR DAMN MIND, GIRL.
GET THE HELL OFF MY LAWN-MOWER.

LOOK, I KNOW EARL COULD BE AN ASSHOLE AND A DAMN CHORE TO LIVE WITH.
BELIEVE ME, I KNOW.
BUT THAT DON'T MEAN YOU CAN JUST TAKE HIS SHIT AS SOON AS HE'S DEAD.

DIDN'T I FUCKIN' TELL YA? YOU BELIEVE THE FUCKIN' BALLS ON THIS ONE?
BITCH CAME LOOKING FOR TROUBLE. BITCH FOUND IT.
Jeff
YOU HEARD MY COUSIN, GET THE FUCK OFF THE--

HKK
HNG

GGH

UH...

DON'T GO LOSING YOUR NERVE NOW, ASSHOLE.
C'MON. I NEED THIS.
I GOTTA GET THIS SHIT OUTTA MY SYSTEM.
FKK
HPPP
THUMKT
THUMKT
THUMKT

YOU FUCKIN' CUNT!
DON'T YOU TOUCH MY FUCKIN' MAN, YOU FUCKIN' CUNT!
I'LL CUT YOUR FUCKIN'...

HEY, LITTLE MAN. WILLIE, AIN'T IT?
WHY DON'T YOU GO FETCH US A SWITCH OFF THE TREE, WILLIE.
A REAL BIG ONE FOR YOUR DAD HERE.
SLAP!

I AIN'T GOTTA DO WHAT NO NIGGER TELLS ME.

EVER SINCE I CAME BACK HERE...I'VE BEEN TRYING TO TELL MYSELF IT DON'T MATTER.

IT'S JUST BIOLOGY. IT DON'T DEFINE YOU. IT DON'T MAKE YOU WHO YOU ARE, NOT REALLY.
BUT THAT'S WRONG.
I WAS COMPLETELY GODDAMN WRONG.

IT DOES MATTER.
MAYBE NOT TO EVERYBODY ELSE.
BUT IT FUCKING MATTERS TO ME.
MORE THAN I EVER THOUGHT IT DID.

IT MATTERS WHO YOUR DADDY IS.
Momma
00:18
CALLING...
HEY, MOMMA.
YEAH, SORRY.

NO, LISTEN, MOMMA... I...
NO, JUST... NO, THERE'S NO POINT IN...
DAMNIT, MOMMA, SHUT UP AND LISTEN FOR A SECOND, PLEASE!

I NEED TO KNOW WHAT THE COPS TOLD YOU.
EVERYTHING THEY TOLD YOU.

"I NEED TO KNOW HOW DADDY *DIED*."

WELCOME TO
CRAW COUNTY
HOME OF THE 5-TIME
STATE 4A FOOTBALL
CHAMPION
RUNNIN' REBS

SOUTHERN BASTARDS

Cover Gallery & Sketchbook

JASON AARON JASON LATOUR

SOUTHERN BASTARDS

JASON AARON JASON LATOUR

SOUTHERN BASTARDS

Issue 9 variant by
TONY MOORE

JASON AARON JASON LATOUR

SOUTHERN BASTARDS

REBEL

JASON AARON JASON LATOUR

SOUTHERN BASTARDS

JASON AARON JASON LATOUR

SOUTHERN BASTARDS

JASON LATOUR CHRIS BRUNNER

SOUTHERN BASTARDS

JASON AARON
JASON LATOUR

JASON AARON JASON LATOUR

SOUTHERN BASTARDS

MOTHER EMANUEL HOPE FUND

Charity Variant.

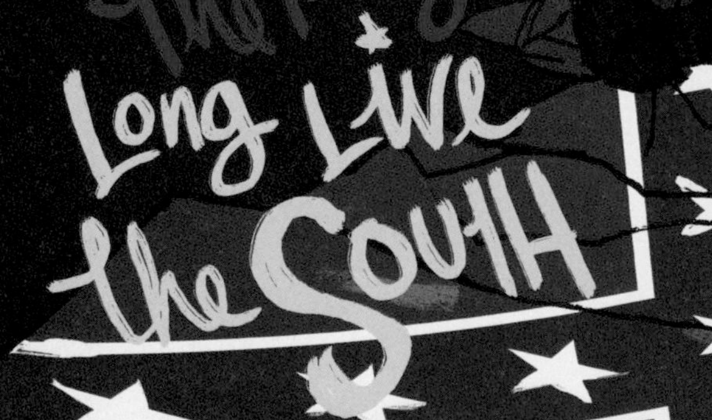

JASON AARON JASON LATOUR

SOUTHERN BASTARDS

ON THE REBEL FLAG...

By Jason Latour

As you can imagine, I've heard a lot of feedback about our variant cover to SOUTHERN BASTARDS #10. While a great deal of it was positive encouragement-- I still feel a great need to expound upon why I'm taking such a hard line on this topic. Being a Southerner is very important to me. It is my culture, and by and large, it's been very rewarding to me over the course of my life. Though I can't speak for him, I think it's been equally so for Jason Aaron.

So I'm writing this in part because I do take this issue seriously, and I want it to to be clear that even though my cover might be seen as a touch sensational-- it was not something that was waded into casually. We knew that a dog tearing up the Confederate flag was not the most subtle of images, but as far as the discourse on this topic goes it seemed fitting. It's never been all that subtle of a conversation has it?

And now that I (hopefully) have your attention I want to admit something to you-- I'm a white man from the South. Charlotte, North Carolina in fact. A place an hour removed from all the noise down in Columbia, SC. A couple more from those horrific murders in Charleston. I'm a white Southern man who, despite my harsh objections to what I feel it represents, is willing to admit that I have a conflicted relationship with the Confederate flag.

No big news story there. There's definitely nothing novel about being conflicted as a Southerner. As we all know that everywhere we go, we're recognized by some stereotypical aspect of our heritage. Be that our accent or our taste in music or the assumption that we might be a little backwards, a little slow. Many of us spend a lot of time challenging or fighting these assertions. Some of us run from them. It's my feeling that the best of us own them. We admit when mistakes were made. We fight like hell when we're right. Twice as hard when we've been wronged. And that's what I see when I look at that flag; when I hear its supporters. I don't hear people who think they're right-- I hear folks who think they've been wronged.

But, why? Where does that come from? Can it be as simple as all the things done, and said those centuries ago still hanging in the air down here? I've asked myself that a lot. And after years of thinking long and hard about it, of punching my fists against the red clay bricks and into humid air-- I really think that's the root of it. Yes, it comes from the past. But it lives in the present. It lives in the inability to reconcile what we want with what is. It's born from human frailty, in the refusal to believe that we're not strong enough to navigate or overcome the chaos of a world we had no choice about being brought into. It comes from believing in a myth. The myth that we're so goddamned important.

But, what does that have to do with the Rebel flag? Phew-- well-- everything I think. But, how do we boil that down, and get to the root of where it all starts? Well, better and brighter minds than I have and will wrestle with it-- but the best I can do is ask that for briefest of moments, let's take a leap, and set aside all the things it's mutated into and appropriated to mean over the last couple centuries or more. The symbolism we're left with is that of a Confederate battle flag. The banner of a defeated nation.

The Civil War was about the abolition of slavery. Perhaps it wasn't about morality, or equality, or the need to do what was right for humankind, but it was about slavery because slavery was power. In the South in the 1800's money came from cotton and cotton came from slaves. So with the entirety of the uncharted west of America unfolding out before them, our government had a choice-- Do we allow slavery to expand? Do we allow aristocrats of the South to expand their influence and power further? Questions the country ultimately went to war to answer.

In many cases, poor whites in the South fought for the interests of the ruling class of Confederate aristocrats. Often their sole motivation being a certain freedom of their own, the promise that one day they too would be able to carve out their own piece of land, or navigate their lives free of another man's will. A dream that in many ways sounds much like the one many Americans still believe in today. Many of them probably carried no hatred in their hearts for another man's skin color, many of them likely saw themselves as trapped by circumstance. If you're from the South, the possibility that a basically good and decent person in your family died under that flag does exist. Throughout history, countless lives have been lost under banners that don't represent their individual beliefs. But racist or not, the men and women that fought and lived under the Confederacy are still complicit. Their own fight to determine their own course came at the expense of another human's freedom.

Which brings me back to the great myth. Crippled, and humiliated in the wake of the war, the promise of riches and freedom and good fortune snatched from the Southern grasp. The promises of the Confederacy in a grave alongside it, all that was left was "The American Dream". A dream that the slaves once chained in the field now had within their grasp as well. All bets were off, anything was possible, and that small shred of petty dignity-- that one assurance that the color of your skin allowed you a chance in the world, was now gone.

It was no doubt a moment of extreme existential confusion-- one that still exists today.

Whites all over began to question their place. If it wasn't next to the boss on the hill, then where was it?

You see racism, in its way, has always been about power more than skin color. Encouraging the people under your heel to quibble and fight amongst themselves is a good way to keep them from banding together to lift your boot off their necks. Racial divisions were encouraged for this reason, and the white need to feel superior, to feel stronger than the slaves chained in the field was encouraged to prevent them from accepting that fences were around them too.

And so that frustration was transferred. With everything about their lives and their place in the world in doubt, many whites struggled to maintain any power they could muster. They used their working knowledge of the world they'd built to limit the opportunities and freedoms of the freed slaves. Despite the fact that much of the South was built by their hands and on their backs, blacks were told often as possible that they were different, lesser, that they didn't belong. Institutional racism took hold.

But there came a time when signs over water fountains and leering glances didn't do it. When black men and women stood up and fought back. When a stronger symbol was needed.

And that's when the Rebel flag came back into the fold. A symbol for the belief that blacks and whites are different. That we have different places in the world. That we are divided. Even if you remove the horrific acts done in its name-- That's what the rebel flag has ALWAYS stood for. It's what it will always stand for.

And that's why it's time for the Rebel flag to disappear.

Not from our history books, or museums or even our works of art or fiction. If you want to wear it on your clothes or hang it in your home, that's your prerogative. But as a symbol of our modern culture-- it has no place.

I understand that you may have a loved one who respected that flag, or that it reminds you of. Maybe there's some deep-seated association that brings you joy. But you need to accept that it has a meaning that goes beyond how you feel. It goes beyond how much you liked Dukes of Hazzard. There are other people it's very existence has long served to do nothing but demean and cause harm. People who've been wronged.

I refuse to believe that Southern pride stems from the pain we've inflicted on others. Southern pride comes from what we've built together. In our music and art and innovation.

In the people who honor us by taking our culture out into the world and celebrating it. It comes from people seeking us out, and flocking here to experience all that we know and love.

We are all neighbors. We are all Southerners. This is OUR culture, and it means what WE choose it to mean.

So, yes. I'll say it again-- Southern Pride is good collard greens.

Death to the flag.

Long live the South.

Earl Tubb sketches by
JASON LATOUR

Earl Tubb sketches by
JASON LATOUR

Issue 12 sketches by
CHRIS BRUNNER

Earl Tubb sketch by
TONCI ZONJIC

Earl Tubb sketch by
DANIEL WARREN JOHNSON

SOUTHERN BASTARDS

coming soon...

Volume 4: **GUT CHECK**